SHADOWS ON THE ROCK

BY WILLA CATHER

SHADOWS
ON
THE
ROCK

VINTAGE BOOKS
A DIVISION OF RANDOM HOUSE
NEW YORK

CONTENTS

BOOK I
THE APOTHECARY

*Vous me demandez des graines de fleurs de ce pays.
Nous en faisons venir de France pour notre jardin, n'y en
ayant pas ici de fort rares ni de fort belles. Tout y est sau-
vage, les fleurs aussi bien que les hommes.*

Marie de l'Incarnation
(LETTRE À UNE DE SES SŒURS)

Québec, le 12 août, 1653

THE APOTHECARY

One afternoon late in October of the year 1697, Euclide Auclair, the philosopher apothecary of Quebec, stood on the top of Cap Diamant gazing down the broad, empty river far beneath him. Empty, because an hour ago the flash of retreating sails had disappeared behind the green island that splits the St. Lawrence below Quebec, and the last of the summer ships from France had started on her long voyage home.

As long as *La Bonne Espérance* was still in sight, many of Auclair's friends and neighbours had kept him company on the hill-top; but when the last tip of white slid behind the curving shore, they went back to their shops and their kitchens to face the stern realities of life. Now for eight months the French colony on this rock in the North would be entirely cut off from Europe, from the world. This was October; not a sail would come up that wide waterway before next July. No supplies; not a cask of wine or a sack of flour, no gunpowder, or leather, or cloth, or iron tools. Not a letter, even—no news of what went on at home. There might be new wars, floods, conflagrations, epidemics, but the colonists would never know of them until next summer. People sometimes said that if King Louis died, the Minister would send word by the English ships that came to New York all winter, and the Dutch traders at Fort Orange would dispatch couriers to Montreal.

The apothecary lingered on the hill-top long after his fellow townsmen had gone back to their affairs; for him this severance from the world grew every year harder to bear. It was a strange thing, indeed, that a man of his mild and thoughtful disposition, city-bred and most conventional in his habits, should be found on a grey rock in the Canadian wilderness. Cap Diamant, where he stood, was merely the highest ledge of that fortified cliff which was "Kebec,"—a triangular headland wedged in by the joining of two rivers, and girdled about by the greater river as by an encircling arm. Directly under his feet was the French stronghold,—scattered spires and slated roofs flashing in the rich, autumnal sunlight; the little capital which was just then the subject of so much discussion in Europe, and the goal of so many fantastic dreams.

Auclair thought this rock-set town like nothing so much as one of those little artificial mountains which were

4

made in the churches at home to present a theatric scene of the Nativity; cardboard mountains, broken up into cliffs and ledges and hollows to accommodate groups of figures on their way to the manger; angels and shepherds and horsemen and camels, set on peaks, sheltered in grottoes, clustered about the base.

Divest your mind of Oriental colour, and you saw here very much such a mountain rock, cunningly built over with churches, convents, fortifications, gardens, following the natural irregularities of the headland on which they stood; some high, some low, some thrust up on a spur, some nestling in a hollow, some sprawling unevenly along a declivity. The Château Saint-Louis, grey stone with steep dormer roofs, on the very edge of the cliff overlooking the river, sat level; but just beside it the convent and church of the Récollet friars ran downhill, as if it were sliding backwards. To landward, in a low, well-sheltered spot, lay the Convent of the Ursulines ... lower still stood the massive foundation of the Jesuits, facing the Cathedral. Immediately behind the Cathedral the cliff ran up sheer again, shot out into a jutting spur, and there, high in the blue air, between heaven and earth, rose old Bishop Laval's Seminary. Beneath it the rock fell away in a succession of terraces like a circular staircase; on one of these was the new Bishop's new Palace, its gardens on the terrace below.

Not one building on the rock was on the same level with any other,—and two hundred feet below them all was the Lower Town, crowded along the narrow strip of beach between the river's edge and the perpendicular face of the cliff. The Lower Town was so directly underneath the Upper Town that one could stand on the terrace of the Château Saint-Louis and throw a stone down into the narrow streets below.

These heavy grey buildings, monasteries and churches, steep-pitched and dormered, with spires and slated roofs, were roughly Norman Gothic in effect. They were made by people from the north of France who knew no other way of building. The settlement looked like something cut off from one of the ruder towns of Normandy or Brittany, and brought over. It was indeed a rude beginning of a "new France," of a Saint-Malo or Rouen or Dieppe, anchored here in the ever-changing northern light and weather. At its feet, curving about its base, flowed the mighty St. Lawrence, rolling north toward the purple line of the Laurentian mountains, toward frowning Cap Tourmente which rose dark against the soft blue of the October sky. The Île d'Orléans, out in the middle of the river, was like a hilly map, with downs and fields and pastures lying in folds above the naked tree-tops.

On the opposite shore of the river, just across from the proud rock of Quebec, the black pine forest came down to the water's edge; and on the west, behind the town, the forest stretched no living man knew how far. That was the dead, sealed world of the vegetable kingdom, an uncharted continent choked with interlocking trees, living, dead, half-dead, their roots in bogs and swamps, strangling each other in a slow agony that had lasted for centuries. The forest was suffocation, annihilation; there European man was quickly swallowed up in silence, distance, mould, black mud, and the stinging swarms of insect life that bred in it. The only avenue of escape was along the river. The river was the one thing that lived, moved, glittered, changed,—a highway along which men could travel, taste the sun and open air, feel freedom, join their fellows, reach the open sea . . . reach the world, even!

After all, the world still existed, Auclair was thinking, as he stood looking up the way by which *La Bonne Espérance* had gone out only an hour ago. He was not of the proper stuff for a colonist, and he knew it. He was a slender, rather frail man of about fifty, a little stooped, a little grey, with a short beard cut in a point, and a fair complexion delicately flushed with pink about his cheeks and ears. His blue eyes were warm and interested, even in reflection,—they often had a kindling gleam as if his thoughts were pictures. Except for this lively and inquiring spirit in his glance, everything about him was modest and retiring. He was clearly not a man of action, no Indian-fighter or explorer. The only remarkable thing about his life was that he had not lived it to the end exactly where his father and grandfather had lived theirs,—in a little apothecary shop on the Quai des Célestins, in Paris.

The apothecary at last turned his back to the river. He

was glancing up at the sun to reckon the time of day, when he saw a soldier coming up the grassy slope of Cap Diamant by the irregular earth path that led to the redoubt. The soldier touched his hat and called to him.

"I thought I recognized your figure up here, Monsieur Euclide. The Governor requires your presence and has sent a man down to your shop to fetch you."

Auclair thanked him for his trouble and went down the hill with him to the Château. The Governor was his patron, the Count de Frontenac, in whose service he had come out to Canada.

II

It was late in the afternoon when Auclair left the Château and made his way through the garden of the Récollet friars, past the new Bishop's Palace, and down to his own house. He lived on the steep, winding street called Mountain Hill, which was the one and only thoroughfare connecting the Upper Town with the Lower. The Lower Town clustered on the strip of beach at the foot of the cliff, the Upper Town crowned its summit. Down the face of the cliff there was but this one path, which had probably been a mere watercourse when Champlain and his men first climbed up it to plant the French lilies on the crest of the naked rock. The watercourse was now a steep, stony street, with shops on one side and the retaining walls of the Bishop's Palace on the other. Auclair lived there for two reasons: to be close at hand where Count Frontenac could summon him quickly to the Château, and because, thus situated on the winding stairway connecting the two halves of Quebec, his services were equally accessible to the citizens of both.

On entering his door the apothecary found the front shop empty, lit by a single candle. In the living-room behind, which was partly shut off from the shop by a partition made of shelves and cabinets, a fire burned in the fireplace, and the round dining-table was already set with a white cloth, silver candlesticks, glasses, and two clear decanters, one of red wine and one of white.

Behind the living-room there was a small, low-roofed kitchen, built of stone, though the house itself was built of wood in the earliest Quebec manner,—double walls, with sawdust and ashes filling in the space between the two frames, making a protection nearly four feet thick against the winter cold. From this stone kitchen at the back two pleasant emanations greeted the chemist: the rich odour of roasting fowl, and a child's voice, singing. When he closed the heavy wooden door behind him, the voice called: "Is it you, Papa?"

His daughter ran in from the kitchen,—a little girl of twelve, beginning to grow tall, wearing a short skirt and a sailor's jersey, with her brown hair shingled like a boy's. Auclair stooped to kiss her flushed cheek. *"Pas de clients?"* he asked.

"*Mais, oui! Beaucoup de clients.* But they all wanted very simple things. I found them quite easily and made notes of them. But why were you gone so long? Is Monsieur le Comte ill?"

"Not ill, exactly, but there is troublesome news from Montreal."

"Please change your coat now, Papa, and light the candles. I am so anxious about the poulet. Mère Laflamme tried hard to sell me a cock, but I told her my father always complained of a cock." The daughter's eyes were shaped like her father's, but were much darker, a very dark blue, almost black when she was excited, as she was now about the roast. Her mother had died two years ago, and she made the ménage for her father.

Contrary to the custom of his neighbours, Auclair dined at six o'clock in winter and seven in summer, after the day's work was over, as he was used to do in Paris,— though even there almost everyone dined at midday. He now dropped the curtains over his two shop windows, a sign to his neighbours that he was not to be disturbed unless for serious reasons. Having put on his indoor coat, he lit the candles and carried in the heavy soup tureen for his daughter.

They ate their soup in appreciative silence, both were a little tired. While his daughter was bringing in the roast, Auclair poured a glass of red wine for her and one of white for himself.

"Papa," she said as he began to carve, "what is the

earliest possible time that Aunt Clothilde and Aunt Blanche can get our letters?"

Auclair deliberated. Every fall the colonists asked the same question of one another and reckoned it all anew. "Well, if *La Bonne Espérance* has good luck, she can make La Rochelle in six weeks. Of course, it has been done in five. But let us say six; then, if the roads are bad, and they are likely to be in December, we must count on a week to Paris."

"And if she does not have good luck?"

"Ah, then who can say? But unless she meets with very heavy storms, she can do it in two months. With this west wind, which we can always count on, she will get out of the river and through the Gulf very speedily, and that is sometimes the most tedious part of the voyage. When we came over with the Count, we were a month coming from Percé to Quebec. That was because we were sailing against this same autumn wind which will be carrying *La Bonne Espérance* out to sea."

"But surely the aunts will have our letters by New Year's, and then they will know how glad I was of my béret and my jerseys, and how we can hardly wait to open the box upstairs. I can remember my Aunt Blanche a little, because she was young and pretty, and used to play with me. I suppose she is not young now, any more; it is eight years."

"Not young, exactly, but she will always have high spirits. And she is well married, and has three children who are a great joy to her."

"Three little cousins whom I have never seen, and one of them is named for me! Cécile, André, Rachel." She spoke their names softly. These little cousins were almost like playfellows. Their mother wrote such long letters about them that Cécile felt she knew them and all their ways, their individual faults and merits. Cousin Cécile was seven, very studious, *bien sérieuse*, already prepared for confirmation; but she would eat only sweets and highly spiced food. André was five, truthful and courageous, but he bit his nails. Rachel was a baby, in the midst of teething when they last heard of her.

Cécile would have preferred to live with Aunt Blanche and her children when she should go back to France; but by her mother's wish she was destined for Aunt Clothilde, who had long been a widow of handsome means and was much interested in the education of young girls. The face of this aunt Cécile could never remember, though she could see her figure clearly,—standing against the light, she always seemed to be, a massive woman, short and heavy though not exactly fat,—square, rather, like a great piece of oak furniture; always in black, widow's black that smelled of dye, with gold rings on her fingers and a very white handkerchief in her hand. Cécile could see her head, too, carried well back on a short neck, like a general or a statesman sitting for his portrait; but the face was a blank, just as if the aunt were standing in a doorway with blinding sunlight behind her. Cécile was once more trying to recall that face when her father interrupted her.

"What are we having for dessert tonight, my dear?"

"We have the cream cheese you brought from market yesterday, and whichever conserve you prefer; the plums, the wild strawberries, or the gooseberries."

"Oh, the gooseberries, by all means, after chicken."

"But, Papa, you prefer the gooseberries after almost everything! It is lucky for us we can get all the sugar we want from the Count. Our neighbours cannot afford to make conserves, with sugar so dear. And gooseberries take more than anything else."

"There is something very palatable about the flavour of these gooseberries, a bitter tang that is good for one. At home the gooseberries are much larger and finer, but I have come to like this bitter taste."

"*En France nous avons tous les légumes, jusqu'aux dattes,*" murmured Cécile. She had never seen a date, but she had learned that phrase from a book, when she went to day-school at the Ursulines.

Immediately after dinner the apothecary went into the front shop to post his ledger, while his daughter washed the dishes with the hot water left in an iron kettle on the stove, where the birch-wood fire was now smouldering coals. She had scarcely begun when she heard a soft scratching at the single window of her kitchen. Through the small panes of glass a face was looking in,—a terrifying face, but one that she expected. She nodded and beckoned with her finger. A short, heavy man shuffled into the kitchen. He seemed loath to enter, yet drawn by some desire stronger than his reluctance. Cécile went to the stove and filled a bowl.

"There is your soup for you, Blinker."

"Merci, Ma'm'selle." The man spoke out of the side of his mouth, as he looked out of the side of his face. He was so terribly cross-eyed that Cécile had never really looked into his eyes at all,—this was why he was called Blinker. He took a half-loaf from his coat-pocket and began to eat the soup eagerly, trying not to make a noise. Eating was difficult for him,—he had once had an abscess in his lower jaw, it had suppurated, and pieces of the bone had come out. His face was badly shrunken on that side, under the old scars. He knew it distressed Cécile if he gurgled his soup; so he struggled between greed and caution, dipping his bread to make it easy chewing.

This poor mis-shapen fellow worked next door, tended the oven fires for Nicholas Pigeon, the baker, so that the baker could get his night's sleep. His wages were the baker's old clothes, two pairs of boots a year, a pint of red wine daily, and all the bread he could eat. But he got no soup there, Madame Pigeon had too many children to feed.

When he had finished his bowl and loaf, he rose and without saying anything took up two large wooden pails. One was full of refuse from the day's cooking, the other full of dish-water. These he carried down Mountain Hill, through the market square to the edge of the shore, and there emptied them into the river. When he came back, he found a very small glass of brandy waiting for him on the table.

"Merci, Ma'm'selle, merci beaucoup," he muttered. He sat down and sipped it slowly, watching Cécile arrange the kitchen for the night. He lingered while the floor was swept, the last dish put in place on the shelves, the dish-towels hung to dry on a wire above the stove, following all these operations intently with his crooked eyes. When she took up her candle, he must go. He put down his glass, got up, and opened the back door, but his feet seemed nailed to the sill. He stood blinking with that incredibly stupid air, blinking out of the side of his face, and Cécile could not be sure that he saw her or anything else. He made a fumbling as if to button his coat, though there were no buttons on it.

"Bon soir, Ma'm'selle," he muttered.

Since this happened every night, Cécile thought nothing of it. Her mother had begun to look out for Blinker a little before she became so ill, and he was one of the cares the daughter had inherited. He had come out to the colony four years ago, and like many others who came he had no trade. He was strong, but so ill-favoured that nobody wanted him about. Neighbour Pigeon found he was faithful and dependable, and taught him to stoke the wood fire and tend the oven between midnight and morning. Madame Auclair felt sorry for the poor fellow and got into the way of giving him his soup at night and letting him do the heavy work, such as carrying in wood and water and taking away the garbage. She had always called Blinker by his real name, Jules. He had a cave up in the rocky cliff behind the bakery, where he kept his chest,—he slept there in mild weather. In winter he slept anywhere about the ovens that he could find room to lie down, and his clothes and woolly red hair were usually white with ashes. Many people were afraid of him, felt that he must have crooked thoughts behind such crooked eyes. But the Pigeons and Auclairs had got used to him and saw no harm in him. The baker said he could never discover how the fellow made a living at home, or why he had come out to Canada. Many unserviceable men had come, to be sure, but they were usually adventurers who disliked honest work,—wanted to fight the Iroquois or traffic in beaver-skins, or live a free life hunting game in the woods. This Blinker had never had a gun in his hands. He had such a horror of the forest that he would not even go into the near-by woods to help fell trees for firewood, and his fear of Indians was one of the bywords of Mountain Hill. Pigeon used to tell his customers that if the Count went to chastise the Iroquois beyond Cataraqui, Blinker would hide in his cave in Quebec. Blinker protested he had been warned in a dream that he would be taken prisoner and tortured by the Indians.

Dinner was the important event of the day in the apothecary's household. The luncheon was a mere goûter. Breakfast was a pot of chocolate, which he prepared very carefully himself, and a fresh loaf which Pigeon's oldest boy brought to the door. But his dinner Auclair regarded

as the thing that kept him a civilized man and a Frenchman. It put him in a mellow mood, and he and his daughter usually spent the long evening very happily without
visitors. She read aloud to him, the fables of La Fontaine
or his favourite Plutarch, and he corrected her accent
so that she would not be ashamed when she returned
home to the guardianship of that intelligent and exacting
Aunt Clothilde. It was only in the evening that her father
had time to talk to her. All day he was compounding
remedies, or visiting the sick, or making notes for a work
on the medicinal properties of Canadian plants which he
meant to publish after his return to Paris. But in the evening he was free, and while he enjoyed his Spanish snuff
their talk would sometimes lead far away and bring out
long stories of the past. Her father would try to recall to
her their old shop on the Quai des Célestins, where he
had grown up and where she herself was born. She
thought she could remember it a little, though she was
only four years old when they sailed with the Count for
the New World. It was a narrow wedge, that shop, built
in next to the carriage court of the town house of the
Frontenacs. Auclair's little chamber, where he slept from
his sixth year until his marriage, was on the third floor,
under the roof. Its one window looked out upon the
carriage court and across it to the front of the mansion,
which had only a blind wall on the street and faced upon
its own court.

When he was a little boy, he used to tell Cécile, nothing

ever changed next door, except that after a rain the cobbles
in the yard were whiter, and the ivy on the walls was
greener. Every morning he looked out from his window on the same stillness; the shuttered windows behind
their iron grilles, the steps under the porte-cochère green
with moss, pale grass growing up between the stones in
the court, the empty stables at the back, the great wooden
carriage gates that never opened,—though in one of
them a small door was cut, through which the old care-
taker came and went.

"Naturally," Auclair would tell his daughter, "having
seen the establishment next door always the same, I supposed it was meant to be like that, and was there, perhaps,
to give a little boy the pleasure of watching the swallows
build nests in the ivy. The Count had been at home when
I was an infant in arms, and once, I believe, when I was
three, but I could not remember. Imagine my astonishment when, one evening about sunset, a dusty coach with
four horses rattled down the Quai and stopped at the
carriage entrance. Two footmen sprang down from the
box, rang the outer bell, and, as soon as the bar was
drawn, began pulling and prying at the gates, which I
had never seen opened in my life. It seemed to me that
some outrage was being committed and the police should
be called. At last the gates were dragged inward, and the
coach clattered into the court. If anything more happened
that night I do not recall it.

"The next morning I was awakened by shouting under

my window, and the sound of shutters being taken down. I ran across my room and peeped out. The windows over there were not only unshuttered, but open wide. Three young men were leaning out over the grilles beating rugs, shaking carpets and wall-hangings into the air. In a moment a blacksmith came in his leather apron, with a kit of tools, and began to repair the hinges of the gates. Boys were running in and out, bringing bread, milk, poultry, sacks of grain and hay for the horses. When I went down to breakfast, I found my father and mother and grandparents all very much excited and pleased, talking a great deal. They already knew in which chamber the Count had slept last night, the names of his equerries, what he had brought with him for supper in a basket from Fontainebleau, and which wines old Joseph had got up from the cellar for him. I had scarcely ever heard my family talk so much.

"Not long after breakfast the Count himself came into our shop. He greeted my father familiarly and began asking about the people of the Quarter as if he had been away only a few weeks. He inquired for my mother and grandmother, and they came to pay their respects. I was pulled out from under the counter where I had hidden, and presented to him. I was frightened because he was wearing his uniform and such big boots. Yes, he was a fine figure of a man forty years ago, but even more restless and hasty than he is now. I remember he asked me if I wanted to be a soldier, and when I told him that I meant to be an apothecary like my father, he laughed and gave me a silver piece."

Though Auclair so often talked to his daughter of the past, it was not because there was nothing happening in the present. At that time the town of Quebec had fewer than two thousand inhabitants, but it was always full of jealousies and quarrels. Ever since Cécile could remember, there had been a feud between Count Frontenac and old Bishop Laval. And now that the new Bishop, Monseigneur de Saint-Vallier, had just come back from France after a three years' absence, the Count was quarrelling with him! Then there was always the old quarrel between the two Bishops themselves, which had broken out with fresh vigour upon de Saint-Vallier's return. Everyone in the diocese took sides with one prelate or the other. Since he landed in September, scarcely a week went by that Monseigneur de Saint-Vallier did not wreck some cherished plan of the old Bishop.

Before they went to bed, Auclair and his daughter usually took a walk. The apothecary believed this habit conducive to sound slumber. Tonight, as they stepped out into the frosty air and looked up, high over their heads, on the edge of the sheer cliff, the Château stood out against the glittering night sky, the second storey of the south wing brilliantly lighted.

"I suppose the Count's candles will burn till long past midnight," Cécile remarked.

"Ah, the Count has many things to trouble him. The King has not been very generous in rewarding his services in the last campaign. Besides, he is old, and the old do not sleep much."

As they climbed Mountain Hill, they passed in front of Monseigneur de Saint-Vallier's new episcopal Palace, and that, too, was ablaze with lights. Cécile longed to see inside that building, toward which the King himself had given fifteen thousand francs. It was said that Monseigneur had brought back with him a great many fine pieces of furniture and tapestry to furnish it. But he was not fond of children, as the old Bishop was, and his servants were very strict, and there seemed to be no way in which one could get a peep behind those heavy curtains at the windows.

Their walk was nearly always the same. On a precipitous rock, scored over with dark, uneven streets, there were not many ways where one could stroll with a careless foot after nightfall. When the wind was not too biting, they usually took the path up to the redoubt on Cap Diamant and looked down over the sleeping town and the great pale avenue of river, with black forest stretching beyond it to the sky. From there the Lower Town was a mere sprinkle of lights along the water's edge. The rock-top, blocked off in dark masses that were convents and churches and gardens, was now sunk in sleep. The only lighted windows to be seen were in the Château, in the Bishop's Palace, and on the top floor of old

Bishop Laval's Seminary, out there on its spur overhanging the river. That top floor, the apothecary told his daughter, was the library, and likely enough some young Canadian-born Seminarians to whom Latin came hard were struggling with the Church Fathers up there.

III

Auclair did a good trade in drugs and herbs and remedies of his own compounding, but his pay was small, and very little of it was in money. Besides, people wasted a great deal of his time in conversation and thus interfered with his study of Canadian plants. Like most philosophers, he was not averse to discourse, but here much of the talk was gossip and very trivial. The colonists liked to drop in at his house upon the slightest pretext; the interior was like home to the French-born. On a heavy morning, when clouds of thick grey fog rolled up from the St. Lawrence, it cheered one to go into a place that was like an apothecary's shop at home; to glimpse the comfortable sitting-room through the tall cabinets and chests of drawers that separated without entirely shutting it off from the shop.

Euclide Auclair had come over with the Count de Frontenac eight years ago, as his apothecary and physician, and had therefore been able to bring whatever he liked of his personal possessions. He came with a full supply of drugs and specifics, his distilling apparatus,

mortars, balances, retorts, and carboys, all the para-
phernalia of his trade, even the stuffed baby alligator,
brought long ago to Paris by some sailor from the West
Indies and purchased by Auclair's grandfather to orna-
ment the shop on the Quai des Célestins.

Madame Auclair had brought her household goods,
without which she could not imagine life at all, and the
salon behind the shop was very much like their old salon
in Paris. There was the same well-worn carpet, made at
Lyon, the walnut dining-table, the two large arm-chairs
and high-backed sofa upholstered in copper-red cotton-
velvet, the long window-curtains of a similar velvet
lined with brown. The same candelabra and china shepherd boy sat on the mantel, the same colour prints of
pastoral scenes hung on the walls. Madame had brought
out to Canada the fine store of linen that had been her
marriage portion, her feather beds and coverlids and
down pillows. As long as she lived, she tried to make the
new life as much as possible like the old. After she began
to feel sure that she would never be well enough to return to France, her chief care was to train her little daughter so that she would be able to carry on this life and this
order after she was gone.

Madame Auclair had kept upon her feet until within a
few weeks of her death. When a spasm of coughing came
on (she died of her lungs) and she was forced to lie down
on the red sofa there under the window, she would
beckon Cécile to the footstool beside her. After she got

her breath again and was resting, she would softly explain many things about the ménage.

"Your father has a delicate appetite," she would murmur, "and the food here is coarse. If it is not very carefully prepared, he will not eat and will fall ill. And he cannot sleep between woollen coverlids, as many people do here; his skin is sensitive. The sheets must be changed every two weeks, but do not try to have them washed in the winter. I have brought linen enough to last the winter through. Keep folding the soiled ones away in the cold upstairs, and in April, when the spring rains come and all the water-barrels are full of soft rain-water, have big Jeanette come in and do a great washing; give the house up to her, and let her take several days to do her work. Beg her to iron the sheets carefully. They are the best of linen and will last your lifetime if they are well treated."

Madame Auclair never spoke of her approaching death, but would say something like this:

"After a while, when I am too ill to help you, you will perhaps find it fatiguing to do all these things alone, over and over. But in time you will come to love your duties, as I do. You will see that your father's whole happiness depends on order and regularity, and you will come to feel a pride in it. Without order our lives would be disgusting, like those of the poor savages. At home, in France, we have learned to do all these things in the best way, and we are conscientious, and that is why we are called the most civilized people in Europe and other nations envy us."

After such admonition Madame Auclair would look intently into the child's eyes that grew so dark when her heart was touched, like the blue of Canadian blueberries, indeed, and would say to herself: "*Oui, elle a beaucoup de loyauté.*"

During the last winter of her illness she lay much of the time on her red sofa, that had come so far out to this rock in the wilderness. The snow outside, piled up against the window-panes, made a grey light in the room, and she could hear Cécile moving softly about in the kitchen, putting more wood into the iron stove, washing the casseroles. Then she would think fearfully of how much she was entrusting to that little shingled head; something so precious, so intangible; a feeling about life that had come down to her through so many centuries and that she had brought with her across the wastes of obliterating, brutal ocean. The sense of "our way,"—that was what she longed to leave with her daughter. She wanted to believe that when she herself was lying in this rude Canadian earth, life would go on almost unchanged in this room with its dear (and, to her, beautiful) objects; that the proprieties would be observed, all the little shades of feeling which make the common fine. The individuality, the character, of M. Auclair's house, though it appeared to be made up of wood and cloth and glass and a little silver, was really made of very fine moral qualities in two women: the mother's unswerving fidelity to certain traditions, and the daughter's loyalty to her mother's wish.

It was because of these things that had gone before, and the kind of life lived there, that the townspeople were glad of any excuse to stop at the apothecary's shop. Even the strange, bitter, mysterious Bishop Laval (more accusing and grim than ever, now that the new Bishop had returned and so disregarded him) used to tramp heavily into the shop for calomel pills or bandages for his varicose legs, and peer, not unkindly, back into the living-room. Once he had asked for a sprig from the box of parsley that was kept growing there even in winter, and carried it away in his hand,—though, as everyone knew, he denied himself all the comforts of the table and ate only the most wretched and unappetizing food.

In a corner, concealed from the shop by tall cabinets, and well away from the window draughts, stood M. Auclair's four-post bed, with heavy hangings. Underneath it was a child's bed, pulled out at night, where Cécile still slept in cold weather. Sometimes on a very bitter night, when the grip of still, intense cold tightened on the rock as if it would extinguish the last spark of life, the pharmacist would hear his daughter softly stirring about, moving something, covering something. He would thrust his night-cap out between the curtains and call:

"Qu'est-ce que tu fais, petite?"

An anxious, sleepy voice would reply:

"*Papa, j'ai peur pour le persil.*"

It had never frozen in her mother's time, and it should not freeze in hers.

IV

The accident of being born next the Count de Frontenac's house in Paris had determined Euclide Auclair's destiny. He had grown up a studious, thoughtful boy, assisting his father in the shop. Every afternoon he read Latin with a priest at the Jesuits on the rue Saint-Antoine. Count Frontenac's irregular and unexpected returns to town made the chief variety in his life.

It was usually after some chagrin or disappointment that the Count came back to the Quai des Célestins. Between campaigns he lived at Île Savary, his estate on the Indre, near Blois. But after some slight at Court, or some difficulty with his creditors, he would suddenly arrive at his father's old town house and shut himself up for days, even weeks, seeing no one but the little people of the parish of Saint-Paul. He had few friends of his own station in Paris,—few anywhere. He was a man who got on admirably with his inferiors,—seemed to find among them the only human ties that were of any comfort to him. He was poor, which made him boastful and extravagant, and he had always lived far beyond his means. At Île Savary he tried to make as great a show as people who were much better off than he,—to equal them in hospitality, in dress, gardens, horses and carriages. But when he was in Paris, living among the quiet, faithful people of the quarter, he was a different man. With his humble neighbours his manners were irreproachable. He often dropped in at the pharmacy to see his tenants, the Auclairs, and would sometimes talk to the old grandfather about his campaigns in Italy and the Low Countries.

The Count had begun his military life at fifteen, and wherever there was fighting in Europe, he always managed to be there. In each campaign he added to his renown, but never to his fortune. When his military talents were unemployed, he usually got into trouble of some sort. It was after his Italian campaign, when he was recuperating from his wounds in his father's old house on the Quai, that he made his unfortunate marriage. Euclide's father could remember that affair very well. Madame de la Grange-Frontenac and her husband lived together but a short while,—and now they had been separated for almost a lifetime. She still lived in Paris, with a brilliant circle about her,—had an apartment in the old Arsenal building, not far from the Count's house, and when she received, he sometimes paid his respects with the rest of the world, but he never went to see her privately.

When Euclide was twenty-two, Count Frontenac was employed by the Venetians to defend the island of Crete against the Turks. From that command he returned with great honour, but poorer than ever. For the next three years he was idle. Then, suddenly, the King appointed him Governor General of Canada, and he quitted Europe for ten years.

During that decade Euclide's father and mother died. He married, and devoted himself seriously to his profession. Too seriously for his own good, indeed. Although he was so content with familiar scenes and faces as to be almost afraid of new ones, he was not afraid of new ideas,—or of old ideas that had gone out of fashion because surgeons and doctors were too stupid to see their value. The brilliant reign of Louis XIV was a low period in medicine; dressmakers and tailors were more considered than physicians. Euclide had gone deep into the history of medicine in such old Latin books as were stuffed away in the libraries of Paris. He looked back to the time of Ambroise Paré, and still further back to the thirteenth century, as golden ages in medicine,—and he considered Fagon, the King's physician, a bigoted and heartless quack.

When sick people in his own neighbourhood came to Euclide for help, he kept them away from doctors,—gave them tisanes and herb-teas and poultices, which at least could do no harm. He advised them about their diet; reduced the surfeit of the rich, and prescribed goat's milk for the poorly nourished. He was strongly opposed to indiscriminate blood-letting, particularly to bleeding from the feet. This eccentricity made him very unpopular, not only with the barber-surgeons of the parish, but with their patients, and even estranged his own friends.

Bleeding from the feet was very much in vogue just then; it made a sick man feel that the utmost was being done for him. At Versailles it was regularly practised on members of the King's household. Euclide's opposition to this practice lost him many of his patrons. His neighbours used to laugh and say that whether bleeding from the feet harmed other people or not, it had certainly been very bad for the son of their reliable old pharmacien, Alphonse Auclair.

Euclide's business contracted steadily, so that, with all his wife's good management and his own devotion to his profession, he scarcely knew where to turn; until one day the Count de Frontenac walked into the shop and put out his hand as if to rescue a drowning man. Auclair had never heard of the Count's difficulties with the Jesuits in Canada, and knew nothing about his recall by the King, until he appeared at the shop door that morning, ten years older, but no richer or better satisfied with the world than when he went away.

The Count was out of favour at Versailles, his estate on the Indre had run down during his absence in Canada, and he had not the means to repair it, so he now spent a good deal of time in the house next door. His presence there, and his patronage, eased the strain of the Auclairs' position. Moreover, he restored to Euclide the ten years' rent for the shop, which had been scrupulously paid to the Count's agent while he was away.

The Count was lonely in his town house. Many of his

old acquaintances had accomplished their earthly period and been carried to the Innocents or the churchyard of Saint-Paul while he was far away in Quebec. His wife was still entertaining her friends at her apartment in the old Arsenal, and the Count occasionally went there on her afternoons at home. Time hung heavy on his hands, and he often sent for Euclide to come to him in a professional capacity,—a flimsy pretext, for, though past sixty, the Count was in robust health. Of an evening they would sometimes sit in the Count's library, talking of New France. Frontenac's thoughts were there, and he liked to tell an eager listener about its great lakes and rivers, the climate, the Indians, the forests and wild animals. Often he would dwell upon the explorations and discoveries of his ill-fated young friend Robert Cavelier de La Salle, one of the few men for whom, in his long life, he ever felt a warm affection.

Gradually there grew up in Auclair's mind the picture of a country vast and free. He fell into a habit of looking to Canada as a possible refuge, an escape from the evils one suffered at home, and of wishing he could go there.

This seemed a safe desire to cherish, since it was impossible of fulfilment. Euclide was a natural city-dweller; one of those who can bear poverty and oppression, so long as they have their old surroundings, their native sky, the streets and buildings that have become part of their lives. But though he was a creature of habit and derived an actual pleasure from doing things exactly as he had always done them, his mind was free. He could not shut his eyes to the wrongs that went on about him, or keep from brooding upon them. In his own time he had seen taxes grow more and more ruinous, poverty and hunger always increasing. People died of starvation in the streets of Paris, in his own parish of Saint-Paul, where there was so much wealth. All the while the fantastic extravagances of the Court grew more outrageous. The wealth of the nation, of the grain lands and vineyards and forests of France, was sunk in creating the pleasure palace at Versailles. The richest peers of the realm were ruining themselves on magnificent Court dresses and jewels. And, with so many new abuses, the old ones never grew less; torture and cruel punishments increased as the people became poorer and more desperate. The horrible mill at the Châtelet ground on day after day. Auclair lived too near the prisons of Paris to be able to forget them. In his boyhood a harmless old man who lodged in their own cellar was tortured and put to death at the Châtelet for a petty theft.

One morning, in the summer when Cécile was four years old, Count Frontenac made one of his sudden re-appearances in Paris and sent for Euclide. The King had again appointed him Governor General of Canada, and he would sail in a few weeks. He wished to take Auclair with him as his personal physician. The Count was then seventy years old, and he was as eager to be gone as a young man setting off on his first campaign.

Auclair was terrified. Indeed, he fell ill of fright, and neither ate nor slept. He could not imagine facing any kind of life but the one he had always lived. His wife was much the braver of the two. She pointed out that their business barely made them a livelihood, and that after the Count went away it would certainly decline. Moreover, the Count was their landlord, and he had now decided to sell his town property. Who knew but that the purchaser might prove a hard master,—or that he might not pull down the apothecary shop altogether to enlarge the stables?

V

It was the day after *La Bonne Espérance* had set sail for France. Auclair and his daughter were on their way to the Hôtel Dieu to attend the Reverend Mother, who had sprained her ankle. Quebec is never lovelier than on an afternoon of late October; ledges of brown and lavender clouds lay above the river and the Île d'Orléans, and the red-gold autumn sunlight poured over the rock like a heavy southern wine. Beyond the Cathedral square the two lingered under the allée of naked trees beside the Jesuits' college. These trees were cut flat to form an arbour, the branches interweaving and interlacing like basket-work, and beneath them ran a promenade paved with flat flagstones along which the dry yellow leaves were blowing, giving off a bitter perfume when one trampled them. Cécile loved that allée, because when she was little the Fathers used to let her play there with her skipping-rope,—few spots in Kebec were level enough to jump rope on. Behind the avenue of trees the long stone walls of the monastery—seven feet thick, those walls—made a shelter from the wind; they held the sun's heat so well that it was possible to grow wall grapes there, and purple clusters were cut in September.

Behind the Jesuits' a narrow, twisted, cobbled street dropped down abruptly to the Hôtel Dieu, on the banks of the little river St. Charles. Auclair and his daughter went through the garden into the refectory, where Mother Juschereau de Saint-Ignace was seated, her sprained foot on a stool, directing the work of her novices. She was a little over forty, a woman of strong frame, tall, upright, with a presence that bespoke force rather than reserve; a handsome face,—the large, open features mobile and alert, perhaps a trifle masculine. She was the first Reverend Mother of the foundation who was Canadian-born, and she had been elected to that office when she was but thirty-four years of age. She was a religious of the practical type, sunny and very outright by nature,—enthusiastic, without being given to visions or ecstasies.

As the visitors entered, the Superior made as if to rise, but Auclair put out a detaining hand.

"I am two days late, Reverend Mother. In your mind you have been chiding me for neglect. But it is a busy time for us when the last ships sail. We have many family letters to write; and I examine my stock and make out my order for the drugs I shall need by the first boats next summer."

"If you had not come today, Monsieur Euclide, you would surely have found me on my feet tomorrow. When the Indians have a sprain, in the woods, they bind their leg tightly with deer thongs and keep on the march with their party. And they recover."

"Dear Mother Juschereau, the idea of such treatment is repugnant to me. We are not barbarians, after all."

"But they are flesh and blood; how is it they recover?"

As he pushed back her snow-white skirt a little and began gently to unwind the bandage from her foot, Auclair explained his reasons for believing that the savages were much less sensitive to pain than Europeans. Cécile fell to admiring the work Mother Juschereau had in hand. Her lap and the table beside her were full of scraps of bright silk and velvet and sheets of coloured paper. While she overlooked the young Sisters at their tasks, her fingers were moving rapidly and cleverly, making artificial flowers. She had great skill at this and delighted in it,— it was her one recreation.

"Yes, my dear," she said, "I am making these for the poor country parishes, where they have so little for the altar. These are wild roses, such as I used to gather when I was a child at Beauport. Oh, the wild flowers we have in the fields and prairies about Beauport!"

When he had applied his ointment and bandaged her

foot in fresh linen, the apothecary went off to the hospital medicine room, in charge of Sister Marie Domenica, whom he was instructing in the elements of pharmacy, and Cécile settled herself on the floor at Mother Juschereau's knee. Theirs was an old friendship.

The Reverend Mother (Jeanne Franc Juschereau de la Ferté was her proud name) held rather advanced views on caring for the sick. She did not believe in leaving everything to God, and had availed her hospital of Auclair's skill ever since he first came to Quebec. Quick to detect a trace of the charlatan in anyone, she felt confidence in Auclair because his pretensions were so modest. She addressed him familiarly as "Monsieur Euclide," scolded him for teaching his daughter Latin, and was keenly interested in his study of Canadian plants. Cécile had been coming to the Hôtel Dieu with her father almost every week since she was five years old, and Mother Juschereau always found time to talk to her a little; but today was a very unusual opportunity. The Mother was seldom to be found seated in a chair; when she was not on her knees at her devotions, she was on her feet, hurrying from one duty to another.

"It has been a long while since you told me a story, Reverend Mother," Cécile reminded her.

Mother Juschereau laughed. She had a deep warmhearted laugh, something left over from her country girlhood. "Perhaps I have no more to tell you. You must know them all by this time."

"But there is no end to the stories about Mother Catherine de Saint-Augustin. I can never hear them all."

"True enough, when you speak her name, the stories come. Since I have had to sit here with my sprain, I have been recalling some of the things she used to tell me herself, when I was not much older than you."

While her hands flew among the scraps of colour, Mother Juschereau began somewhat formally:

"Before she had left her fair Normandy (*avant qu'elle ait quitté sa belle Normandie*), while Sister Catherine was a novice at Bayeux, there lived in the neighbourhood a *pécheresse* named Marie. She had been a sinner from her early youth and was so proof against all counsel that she continued her disorders even until an advanced age. Driven out by the good people of the town, shunned by men and women alike, she fell lower and lower, and at last hid herself in a solitary cave. There she dragged out her shameful life, destitute and consumed by a loathsome disease. And there she died; without human aid and without the sacraments of the Church. After such a death her body was thrown into a ditch and buried like that of some unclean animal.

"Now, Sister Catherine, though she was so young and had all the duties of her novitiate to perform, always found time to pray for the souls of the departed, for all who died in that vicinity, whether she had known them in the flesh or not. But for this abandoned sinner she did not pray, believing, as did everyone else, that she was for ever lost.

"Twelve years went by, and Sister Catherine had come to Canada and was doing her great work here. One day, while she was at prayer in this house, a soul from purgatory appeared to her, all pale and suffering, and said:

" 'Sister Catherine, what misery is mine! You commend to God the souls of all those who die. I am the only one on whom you have no compassion.'

" 'And who are you?' asked our astonished Mother Catherine.

" 'I am that poor Marie, the sinner, who died in the cave.'

" 'What,' exclaimed Mother Catherine, 'were you then not lost?'

" 'No, I was saved, thanks to the infinite mercy of the Blessed Virgin.'

" 'But how could this be?'

" 'When I saw that I was about to die in the cave, and knew that I was abandoned and cast out by the world, unclean within and without, I felt the burden of all my sins. I turned to the Mother of God and cried to her: *Queen of Heaven, you are the last refuge of the ruined and the outcast; I am abandoned by all the world; I have no hope but you; you alone have power to reach where I am fallen; Mary, Mother of Jesus, have pity upon me!* The tender Mother of all made it possible for me to repent in that last hour. I died and I was saved. The Holy Mother procured for me the favour of having my punishment abridged, and now only a few masses are required to deliver me from purgatory. I beseech you to have them said for me, and I will never cease my prayers to God and the Blessed Virgin for you.'

"Mother Catherine at once set about having masses said for that poor Marie. Some days later there appeared to her a happy soul, more brilliant than the sun, which smiled and said: 'I thank you, my dear Catherine, I go now to paradise to sing the mercies of God for ever, and I shall not forget to pray for you.'"

Here Mother Juschereau glanced down at the young listener, who had been following her intently. "And now, from this we see—" she went on, but Cécile caught her hand and cried coaxingly,

"*N'expliquez pas, chère Mère, je vous en supplie!*"

Mother Juschereau laughed and shook her finger.

"You always say that, little naughty! *N'expliquez pas!* But it is the explanation of these stories that applies them to our needs."

"Yes, dear Mother. But there comes my father. Tell me the explanation some other day."

Mother Juschereau still looked down into her face, frowning and smiling. It was the kind of face she liked, because there was no self-consciousness in it, and no vanity; but she told herself for the hundredth time: "No, she has certainly no vocation." Yet for an orphan girl, and one so intelligent, there would certainly have been a career among the Hospitalières. She would have loved to train that child for the Sœur Apothicaire of her hospital. Her good sense told her it was not to be. When she talked to Cécile of the missionaries and martyrs, she knew that her words fell into an eager mind; admiration and rapture she found in the girl's face, but it was not the rapture of self-abnegation. It was something very different,—almost like the glow of worldly pleasure. She was convinced that Cécile read altogether too much with her father, and had told him so; asking him whether he had perhaps forgotten that he had a girl to bring up, and not a son whom he was educating for the priesthood.

While her father and Mother Juschereau were going over an inventory of hospital supplies, Cécile went into the chapel to say a prayer for the repose of Mother de Saint-Augustin. There, in the quiet, she soon fell to musing upon the story of that remarkable girl who had braved the terrors of the ocean and the wilderness and come out to Canada when she was barely sixteen years old, and this Kebec was but a naked rock rising out of the dark forest.

Catherine de Saint-Augustin had begun her novitiate with the Hospitalières at Bayeux when she was eleven and a half years of age, and by the time she was fourteen she was already, in her heart, vowed to Canada. The letters and *Relations* of the Jesuit missionaries, eagerly read in all the religious houses of France, had fired her bold imagination, and she begged to be sent to save the souls of the savages. Her superiors discouraged her and forbade her to cherish this desire; Catherine's youth and bodily frailness were against her. But while she went about her tasks in the monastery, this wish, this hope, was always with her. One day when she was peeling vegetables in the novices' refectory, she cut her hand, and, seeing the blood flow, she dipped her finger in it and wrote upon the table:

Je mourrai au Canada
Sœur Saint-Augustin

That table, with its inscription, was still shown at Bayeux as an historic relic.

Though Catherine's desire seemed so far from fulfilment, she had not long to wait. In the winter of 1648, Père Vimont, from the Jesuit mission in Canada, came knocking at the door of the monastère at Bayeux, recruiting sisters for the little foundation of Hospitalières already working in Kebec. Catherine was told that she was too young to go, and her father firmly refused to give his permission. But in her eagerness the girl wrote petition after petition to her Bishop and superiors, and at last her request was brought to the attention of the Queen Mother, Anne of Austria. The Queen's intercession won her father's consent.

When, after a voyage of many months, unparalleled for storms and hardships, Catherine and her companions anchored under the rock of Kebec and were rowed ashore, she fell upon her knees and kissed the earth where she first stepped upon it.

Made Superior of the Hôtel Dieu at an early age, she

died before she was forty. At thirty-seven she had burned her life out in vigils, mortifications, visions, raptures, all the while carrying on a steady routine of manual labour and administrative work, observing the full discipline of her order. For long before her death she was sustained by visions in which the spirit of Father Brébeuf, the martyr, appeared to her, told her of the glories of heaven, and gave her counsel and advice for all her perplexities in this world. It was at the direction of Father Brébeuf, communicated to her in these visions, that she chose Jeanne Franc Juschereau de la Ferté to succeed her as Superior, and trained her to that end. To many people the choice seemed such a strange one that Père Brébeuf must certainly have instigated it. Mother Catherine de Saint-Augustin was slight, nervous, sickly from childhood, yet from childhood precocious and prodigious in everything; always dedicating herself to the impossible and always achieving it; now getting a Queen of France to speak for her, now winning the spirit of the hero priest from paradise to direct and sustain her. And the woman she chose to succeed her was hardy, sagacious, practical, —a *Canadienne*, and the woman for Canada.

BOOK II
CÉCILE AND JACQUES

CÉCILE AND JACQUES

I

On the last Friday of October Auclair went as usual to the market, held in front of Notre Dame de la Victoire, the only church in the Lower Town. All the trade in Quebec went on in the Lower Town, and the principal merchants lived on the market square. Their houses were built solidly around three sides of it, wall against wall, the shops on the ground floor, the dwelling-quarters upstairs. On the fourth side stood the church. The merchants' houses had formerly been of wood, but sixteen years ago, just after the Count de Frontenac was recalled to France, leaving Canada a prey to so many misfortunes, the Lower Town had been almost entirely wiped out by fire. It was rebuilt in stone, to prevent a second disaster. This square, which was the centre of

commerce, now had a look of permanence and stability;
houses with walls four feet thick, wide doorways, deep
windows, steep, slated roofs and dormers. *La Place*, as
it was called, was an uneven rectangle, cobble-paved,
sloping downhill like everything else in Quebec, with
gutters to carry off the rainfall. In the middle was a grass
plot (pitifully small, indeed), protected by an iron fence
and surmounted by a very ugly statue of King Louis.

On market days the space about this iron fence was
considered the right of the countrywomen, who trudged
into Quebec at dawn beside the dogs that drew their
little two-wheeled carts. Against the fence they laid out
their wares; white bodies of dressed ducks and chickens,
sausages, fresh eggs, cheese, butter, and such vegetables
as were in season. On the outer edge of the square the
men stationed their carts, on which they displayed quarters
of fresh pork, live chickens, maple sugar, spruce beer,
Indian meal, feed for cows, and long black leaves of
native tobacco tied in bunches. The fish and eel carts,
because of their smell and slimy drip, had a corner of the
square to themselves, just at the head of La Place Street.
The fishmongers threw buckets of cold water over their
wares at intervals, and usually a group of little boys
played just below, building "beaver-dams" in the gutter
to catch the overflow.

This was an important market day, and Auclair went
down the hill early. The black frosts might set in at any
time now, and today he intended to lay in his winter

supply of carrots, pumpkins, potatoes, turnips, beet-root, leeks, garlic, even salads. On many of the wagons there were boxes full of earth, with rooted lettuce plants growing in them. These the townspeople put away in their cellars, and by tending them carefully and cover-ing them at night they kept green salad growing until Christmas or after. Auclair's neighbour, Pigeon the baker, had a very warm cellar, and he grew little carrots and spinach down there long after winter had set in. The great vaulted cellars of the Jesuits and the Récollet friars looked like kitchen gardens when the world above ground was frozen stark. Careless people got through the winter on smoked eels and frozen fish, but if one were willing to take enough trouble, one could live very well, even in Quebec. It was the long, slow spring, March, April, early May, that tried the patience. By that time the winter stores had run low, people were tired of make-shifts, and still not a bud, not a salad except under cold-frames.

The market was full of wood doves this morning. They were killed in great numbers hereabouts, were sold cheap, and made very delicate eating. Every fall Auclair put down six dozens of them in melted lard. He had six stone jars in his cellar for that purpose, packing a dozen birds to the jar. In this way he could eat fresh game all winter, and, preserved thus, the birds kept their flavour. Frozen venison was all very well, but feathered creatures lost their taste when kept frozen a long while.

Auclair carried his purchases over to the cart of his butter-maker, Madame Renaude. Renaude-le-lièvre, she was called, because she had a hare-lip, and a bristling black moustache as well. She was a big, rough Norman woman, who owned seven cows, was extremely clean about her dairy, and quite the reverse in her conversation. In the town there was keen competition for her wares; but as she was rheumatic, she was more or less in thrall-dom to the apothecary, and seldom failed him.

"Good morning, Madame Renaude. Have you my lard for me this morning, as you promised? I must buy my wood doves today."

"Yes, Monsieur Auclair, and I had to kill my pet pig to get it for you, too; one that had slept under the same roof with me."

She spoke very loud, and the farmer at the next stall made an indecent comment.

"Hold your dirty jaw, Joybert. If I had a bad egg, I'd paste you." Old Joybert squinted and looked the other way. "Yes, Monsieur Auclair, you never saw such lard as he made, as sweet as butter. He made two firkins. Surely you won't need so much,—I can sell it anywhere."

"Yes, indeed, madame, I shall need every bit of it. Six dozen birds I have to put down, and I can't do with less."

"But, monsieur, what do you do with the grease after you take your doves out?"

"Why, some of it we use in cooking, and the rest I think my daughter gives to our neighbours."

"To that Blinker, eh? That's a waste! If you were to bring it back to me, I could easily sell it over again and we could both of us make something. The hunters who come up from Three Rivers in winter carry nothing but cold grease to fill their bellies. You forget you are not in France, monsieur. Here grease is meat, not something to throw to criminals."

"I will consider the matter, madame. Now that I am sure of my lard, I must go and select my birds. Good morning, and thank you."

After he had finished his marketing, Auclair put his basket down on the church steps and went inside to say a prayer. Notre Dame de la Victoire was a plain, solid little church, built of very hard rough stone. It had already stood through one bombardment from the waterside, and was dear to the people for that reason. The windows were narrow and set high, like the windows in a fortress, making an agreeable dusk inside. Occasionally, as someone entered to pray, a flash of sunlight and a buzz of talk came in from the Place, cut off when the door closed again.

While the apothecary was meditating in the hush and dusk of the church, he noticed a little boy, kneeling devoutly at one after another of the Stations of the Cross. He was at once interested, for he knew this child very well; a chunky, rather clumsy little boy of six, unkept and uncared for, dressed in a pair of old sailor's breeches, cut off in the leg for him and making a great bulk of loose cloth about his thighs. His ragged jacket was as much too

49

tight as the trousers were too loose, and this gave him the figure of a salt-shaker. He did not look at Auclair or the several others who came and went, being entirely absorbed in his devotions. His lips moved inaudibly, he knelt and rose slowly, clumsily, very carefully, his cap under his arm. Though all his movements were so deliberate, his attention did not wander,—seemed intently, heavily fixed. Auclair carefully remained in the shadow, making no sign of recognition. He respected the child's seriousness.

This boy was the son of 'Toinette Gaux, a young woman who was quite irreclaimable. Antoinette was Canadian-born; her mother had been one of the "King's Girls," as they were called. Thirty years ago King Louis had sent several hundred young Frenchwomen out to Canada to marry the bachelors of the disbanded regiment of Carignan-Salières. Many of these girls were orphans or poor girls of good character; but some were bad enough, and 'Toinette's mother proved one of the worst. She had one daughter, this 'Toinette,—as pretty and as worthless a girl as ever made eyes at the sailors in any seaport town in France. It once happened that 'Toinette fell in love, and then she made great promises of reform. One of the hands on *La Gironde* had come down with a fever in Quebec and was lying sick in the Hôtel Dieu when his ship sailed for France. After he was discharged from the hospital, he found himself homeless in a frontier town in winter, too weak to work. 'Toinette took him in, drove her old sweethearts away, and married him. But soon after this boy, Jacques, was born, she returned to her old ways, and her husband disappeared. It was thought that his shipmates had hidden him on board *La Gironde* and taken him home.

'Toinette and another woman now kept a sailors' lodging-house in the Lower Town, up beyond the King's warehouses. They were commonly called La Grenouille and L'Escargot, because, every summer, when the ships from France began to come in, they stuck in their window two placards: "FROGS," "SNAILS," to attract the hungry sailors, whether they had those delicacies on hand or not. 'Toinette, called La Grenouille, was still good to look at; yellow hair, red cheeks, lively blue eyes, an impudent red mouth over small pointed teeth, like a squirrel's. Her partner, the poor snail, was a vacant creature, scarcely more than half-witted,—and the hard work, of course, was put off on her.

This unfortunate child, Jacques, in spite of his bad surroundings, was a very decent little fellow. He told the truth, he tried to be clean, he was devoted to Cécile and her father. When he came to their house to play, they endeavoured to give him some sort of bringing-up, though it was difficult, because his mother was fiercely jealous.

It was two years ago, soon after her mother's death, that Cécile had first noticed Jacques playing about the market place, and begun to bring him home with her, wash his face, and give him a piece of good bread to eat.

Auclair thought it natural for a little girl to adopt a friendless child, to want something to care for after having helped to care for her mother so long. But he did not greatly like the idea of anything at all coming from La Grenouille's house to his, and he was determined to deprive Cécile of her playfellow if he saw any signs of his bad blood. Observing the little boy closely, he had come to feel a real affection for him.

Once, not long ago, when the children were having their goûter in the salon, and the apothecary was writing at his desk, he overheard Jacques telling Cécile where he would kick any boy who broke down his beaver-dam, and he used a nasty word.

"Oh, Jacques!" Cécile exclaimed, "that is some horrible word you have heard the sailors say!"

Auclair, glancing through the partition, saw the child's pale face stiffen and his round eyes stare; he said nothing at all, but he looked frightened. The apothecary guessed at once that it was not from a sailor but from La Grenouille herself he had got that expression.

Cécile went on scolding him. "Now I am going to do what the Sisters at the convent do when a child says anything naughty. Come into the kitchen, and I will wash your mouth out with soap. It is the only way to make your mouth clean."

All this time Jacques said nothing. He went obediently into the kitchen with Cécile, and when he came back he was wiping his eyes with the back of his hand.

"Is it gone?" he asked solemnly.

This morning, as Auclair watched Jacques at his devotions, it occurred to him that the boatmen who brought the merchants up from Montreal to see the Count were doubtless staying with La Grenouille. Likely enough something rowdy had gone on there last night, and the little boy felt a need of expiation. The apothecary went out of the church softly and took up his basket. All the way up the hill he wondered why La Grenouille should have a boy like that.

When he reached home, he called Cécile, who was busy in the room upstairs, where she slept until cold weather. As he gave her his basket, he asked her whether she had seen Jacques lately.

"No, I haven't happened to. Why, is anything the matter?"

"Oh, nothing that I know of. But I saw him in church just now, saying his prayers at the Stations of the Cross, and I felt sorry for him. Perhaps he is getting old enough to realize."

"Was he clean, Papa?"

The apothecary shook his head.

"Far from clean. I never saw him so badly off. His toes were sticking out of his shoes, and when he knelt I could see that he had no stockings on."

"Oh, dear, and I have never finished the pair I began for him! Papa, if you were to let me off from reading to you for a few evenings, I could soon get them done."

"But his shoes, daughter! It would be a mere waste to give the child new stockings. And shoes are very dear."

Cécile sat down for a moment and thought, while her father put on his shop apron. "Papa," she said suddenly, "would you allow me to speak to the Count? He is kind to children, and I believe he would get Jacques some shoes."

II

That afternoon Cécile ran up the hill with a light heart. She was always glad of a reason for going to the Château, —often slipped into the courtyard merely to see who was on guard duty. Her little friend Giorgio, the drummer boy, was at his post on the steps before the great door, and the moment he saw Cécile he snatched his drumsticks from his trousers pocket and executed a rapid flourish in the air above his drum, making no noise. Cécile laughed, and the boy grinned. This was an old joke, but they still found it amusing. Giorgio was stationed there to announce the arrival of the commanding officer, and of all distinguished persons, by a flourish on his drum. The drum-call echoed amazingly in the empty court, could be heard even in the apothecary shop down the hill, so that one always knew when the Count had visitors.

Cécile told the soldier on duty that she would like to see Picard, the Count's valet, and while she waited for him, she went up the steps to talk with Giorgio and to ask

him if his cold were better, and when he had last heard
from his mother.

The boy's real name was Georges Million; his family
lived over on the Île d'Orléans, and his father was a
farmer, Canadian-born. But the old grandfather, who was
of course the head of the house, had come from Haute-
Savoie as a drummer in the Carignan-Salières regiment.
He played the Alpine horn as well, and still performed
on the flute at country weddings. This grandson,
Georges, took after him,—was musical and wanted nothing in the world but a soldier's life. When he was fifteen,
he came into Quebec and begged the Governor to let
him enter the native militia. He was very small for his
age, but he was a good-looking boy, and the Count took
him on as a drummer until he should grow tall enough
to enlist. He put him into a blue coat, high boots, and a
three-cornered hat, and stationed him at the door to welcome visitors. For some reason the Count always called
him Giorgio, and that had become his name in Quebec.

Giorgio's life was monotonous; his duties were to keep
clean and trim, and to stand perfectly idle in a draughty
courtyard for hours at a time. There were very few distinguished persons in Quebec, and not all of those were
on calling terms with Count Frontenac. The Intendant,
de Champigny, came to the Château when it was necessary, but his relations with the Count were formal rather
than cordial. Sometimes, indeed, he brought Madame de
Champigny with him, and when they rolled up in their

carrosse, Giorgio had a great opportunity. Old Bishop Laval, who would properly have been announced by the drum, had not crossed the threshold of the Château for years. The new Bishop had called but twice since his return from France. Dollier de Casson, Superior of the Sulpician Seminary at Montreal, was a person to be greeted by the drum, and so was Jacques Le Ber, the rich merchant. Sometimes Daniel du Lhut, the explorer in command of Fort Frontenac, came to Quebec, and, very rarely, Henri de Tonti,—that one-armed hero who had an iron hook in place of a hand. For all Indian chiefs and messengers, too, Giorgio could beat his drum long and loud. This form of welcome was very gratifying to the savages. But often the days passed one after another when the drummer had no one to salute but the officers of the fort, and life was very dull for him.

When a friendly soldier was on guard, Cécile would often run in to give the drummer boy some cardamon seeds or raisins from her father's shop, and to gossip with him for a while. This afternoon their talk was cut short by the arrival of the Count's valet, through whom one approached his master. Picard had been with the Count since the Turkish wars, and Cécile had known him ever since she could remember. He took her by the hand and led her into the Château and upstairs to the Count's private apartment in the south wing.

The apartment was of but two rooms, a dressing-cabinet and a long room with windows on two sides, which was both chamber and study. The Governor was seated at a writing-table in the south end, a considerable distance from his fireplace and his large curtained bed. He was nearly eighty years old, but he had changed very little since Cécile could remember him, except that his teeth had grown yellow. He still walked, rode, struck, as vigorously as ever, and only two years ago he had gone hundreds of miles into the wilderness on one of the hardest Indian campaigns of his life. When Picard spoke to him, he laid down his pen, beckoned Cécile with a long forefinger, put his arm about her familiarly, and drew her close to his side, inquiring about her health and her father's. As he talked to her, his eyes took on a look of uneasy, mocking playfulness, with a slightly sarcastic curl of the lips. Cécile was not afraid of him. He had always been one of the important figures in her life; when she was little she used to like to sit on his knee, because he wore such white linen, and satin waistcoats with jewelled buttons. He took great care of his person when he was at home. Nothing annoyed him so much as his agent's neglecting to send him his supply of lavender-water by the first boat in the spring. It vexed him more than a sharp letter from the Minister, or even from the King.

After replying to his courtesies Cécile began at once: "Monsieur le Comte, you know little Jacques Gaux, the son of La Grenouille?"

The old soldier nodded and sniffed, drooping the lid

slightly over one eye,—an expression of his regard for a large class of women. She understood.

"But he is a good little boy, Monsieur le Comte, and he cannot help it about his mother. You know she neglects him, and just now he is very badly off for shoes. I am knitting him some stockings, but the shoes we cannot manage."

"And if I were to give you an order on the cobbler? That is soon done. It is very nice of you to knit stockings for him. Do you knit your own?"

"Of course, monsieur! And my father's."

The old Count looked at her from out his deep eye-sockets, and felt for the hard spots on her palm. "You are content down there, keeping house for your father? Not much time for play, I take it?"

"Oh, everything we do, my father and I, is a kind of play."

He gave a dry chuckle. "Well said! Everything we do is. It gets rather tiresome,—but not at your age, perhaps. I am very well pleased with you, Cécile, because you do so well for your father. We have too many idle girls in Kebec, and I cannot say that Kebec is exceptional. I have been about the world a great deal, and I have found only one country where the women like to work,— in Holland. They have made an ugly country very pretty." He slipped a piece of money into her hand. "That is for your charities. Get the frog's son what he needs, and Picard will give Noël Pommier an order for his shoes. And is there nothing you would like for yourself? I have never forgot what a brave sailor you were on the voyage over. You cried only once, and that was when we were coming into the Gulf, and a bird of prey swooped down and carried off a little bird that perched on one of our yard-arms. I wish I had some sweetmeats; you do not often pay me a visit."

"Perhaps you would let me look at your glass fruit," Cécile suggested.

The Count got up and led her to the mantelpiece. Between the tall silver candlesticks stood a crystal bowl full of glowing fruits of coloured glass: purple figs, yellow-green grapes with gold vine-leaves, apricots, nectarines, and a dark citron stuck up endwise among the grapes. The fruits were hollow, and the light played in them, throwing coloured reflections into the mirror and upon the wall above.

"That was a present from a Turkish prisoner whose life I spared when I was holding the island of Crete," the Count told her. "It was made by the Saracens. They blow it into those shapes while the glass is melted. Every piece is hollow; that is why they look alive. Here in Canada it reminds one of the South. You admire it?"

"More than anything I have ever seen," said Cécile fervently.

He laughed. "I like it myself, or I should not have taken so much trouble to bring it over. I think I must leave it to you in my will."

"Oh, thank you, monsieur, but it is quite enough to look at it; one would never forget it. It is much lovelier than real fruit." She curtsied and thanked him again and went out softly to where Picard was waiting for her in the hall. She wished that she could some time go there when the Count was away, and look as long as she pleased at the glass fruit and at the tapestries on the walls of the long room. They were from his estate at Île Savary and represented garden scenes. One could study them for hours without seeing all the flowers and figures.

III

The next morning Auclair sent Cécile up to the Ursuline convent with some borax de Venise which the Mother Superior required, and a bottle of asafœtida for one of the Sisters who was ailing. At this time of year Cécile always felt a little homesick for the Sisters and her old life at the Ursuline school. She had left it so early, because of her mother's illness, and she never passed the garden walls without looking wistfully at the tree-tops which rose above them. From her walks on Cap Diamant she could look down into the rectangular courts and see, through the leafless boughs, the rows of dormer windows in the white roofs, each opening into a Sister's bare little room. One teacher she loved better than any of the others: Sister Anne de Sainte-Rose, who taught history and the French language. She was a niece of the Bishop of Tours, had been happily married, and had led a brilliant life in the great world. Only after the death of her young husband and infant son had she become a religious. She had charm and wit and the remains of great beauty— everything that would appeal to a little girl brought up on a rude frontier. Cécile still saw her when she went to the convent on errands, and she was always invited to the little miracle plays which Sister Anne had the *pensionnaires* give at Christmas-time, for the good of their French and their deportment. But her little visits with her teacher were very short,—stolen pleasures. The nuns were always busy, and if you once dropped out of the school life, you could not share it any more.

This morning she did not see Sister Anne at all; and after delivering her packages to Sister Agatha, the porteress, she turned away to enjoy the weather. It was on days like this that she loved her town best. The autumn fog was rolling in from the river so thick that she seemed to be walking through drifts of brown cloud. Only a few roofs and spires stood out in the fog, detached and isolated: the flèche of the Récollet chapel, the slate roof of the Château, the long, grey outline of Bishop Laval's Seminary, floating in the sky. Everything else was blotted out by rolling vapours that were constantly changing in density and colour; now brown, now amethyst, now reddish lavender, with sometimes a glow of orange overhead where the sun was struggling behind the thick weather.

It was like walking in a dream. One could not see the

people one passed, or the river, or one's own house. Not even the winter snows gave one such a feeling of being cut off from everything and living in a world of twilight and miracles. After loitering on her way, she set off for the Lower Town to look for Jacques.

Cécile never on any account went to his mother's house to find him. Sometimes, in searching for him, she went behind the King's warehouses, as far as the stone paving extended. Beyond the paving the strip of beach directly underneath Cap Diamant grew so narrow that there was room for barely a dozen houses to sit in a straight line against the foot of the cliff, and they were the slum of Quebec. Respectability stopped with the cobble-stones.

This morning she did not have to go so far; she found Jacques in a group of little boys who had kindled a fire of sticks at the foot of Notre Dame street, behind the church. Before she came up to the children, a light sprinkle began to fall. In a few seconds all the brownish-lilac masses of vapour melted away, leaving a lead-coloured sky, and the rain came down in streams, like water poured from a great height. Cécile caught Jacques by the arm and ran with him into the church, which had often been a refuge to them in winter. Not that the church was ever heated, but in there one was out of the wind, and perhaps the bright colours made one feel the cold less. This morning the church was empty, except for an old man and three women at their prayers. There were a few benches on either side of the nave, for old people who could not stand during mass, and the children slipped into one of these, sitting close together to keep warm.

"It's been a long time since we were in here together," Cécile whispered.

He nodded.

"But you come in to say your prayers, don't you, every day?"

"I think so," he answered vaguely.

"That is right. I like this church better than any other. Even in the chapel of the Ursulines I don't feel so much at home, though I used to be there every day when I was going to school. This is our own church, isn't it, Jacques?"

He glanced up at her and smiled faintly. This child never looked very well. He was not thin,—rather chunky, on the contrary,—but there was no colour in his cheeks, or even in his lips. That, Cécile knew, was because he wasn't properly nourished.

"You might tell me about some nice saint," said Jacques presently. She began to whisper the story of Saint Anthony of Padua, who stood quite near them, ruddy and handsome, with a sheaf of lilies on one arm and the Holy Child on the other.

It chanced that this one church* in the Lower Town, near Jacques's little world, where he and Cécile had so often made rendezvous, was peculiarly the church of childhood. It had been renamed Notre Dame de la

* The charm of this old church was greatly spoiled by unfortunate alterations in the lighting, made in the autumn of 1929.

Victoire five years ago, after the Count had driven off Sir William Phips's besieging fleet, in recognition of the protection which Our Lady had afforded Quebec in that hour of danger. But originally it was called the Church of the Infant Jesus, and the furnishings and decorations which had been sent over from France were appropriate for a church of that name.

Two paintings hung in the Lady Chapel, both of Sainte Geneviève as a little girl. In one she sat under a tree in a meadow, with a flock of sheep all about her, and a distaff in her hand, while two angels watched her from a distance. In the other she was reading an illuminated scroll,—but here, too, she was in a field and surrounded by her flock.

The high altar was especially interesting to children, though it was not nearly so costly or so beautiful as the altar in the Ursulines' chapel with its delicate gold-work. It was very simple indeed,—but definite. It was a representation of a feudal castle, all stone walls and towers. The outer wall was low and thick, with many battlements; the second was higher, with fewer battlements; the third seemed to be the wall of the palace itself, with towers and many windows. Within the arched gateway (hung with little velvet curtains that were green or red or white according to the day) the Host was kept. Cécile had always taken it for granted that the Kingdom of Heaven looked exactly like this from the outside and was surrounded by just such walls; that this altar was a reproduction of it, made in France by people who knew; just as the statues of the saints and of the Holy Family were portraits. She had taught Jacques to believe the same thing, and it was very comforting to them both to know just what Heaven looked like,—strong and unassailable, wherever it was set among the stars.

Out of this walled castle rose three tall stone towers, with holy figures on them. On one stood a grave Sainte Anne, regally clad like a great lady of this world, with a jewelled coronet upon her head. On her arm sat a little dark-skinned Virgin, her black hair cut straight across the back like a scholar's, her hands joined in prayer. Sainte Anne was noble in bearing, but not young; her delicately featured face was rather worn by life, and sad. She seemed to know beforehand all the sorrows of her own family, and of the world it was to succour.

On the central tower, which was the tallest and rose almost to the roof of the church, the Blessed Mother and Child stood high up among the shadows. Today, with the leaden sky and floods of rain, it was too dark up there to see her clearly; but the children thought they saw her, because they knew her face so well. She was by far the loveliest of all the Virgins in Kebec, a charming figure of young motherhood,—oh, very young, and radiantly happy, with a stately crown, and a long, blue cloak that parted in front over a scarlet robe. The little Jesus on her arm was not a baby,—he looked as if he would walk if she put him down, and walk very well. He was so intelligent and gay, a child in a bright and joyful mood, both arms outstretched in a gesture of welcome, as if he were giving a fête for his little friends and were in the act of receiving them. He was a little Lord indeed, in his gaiety and graciousness and savoir-faire.

The rain fell on the roof and drove against the windows. Outside, the ledges of bare rock and all the sloping streets were running water; everything was slippery and shiny with wet. The children sat contentedly in their corner, feeling the goodness of shelter. Jacques remarked that it would be nice if there were more candles. The tapers on the votive candle-stand were burning low, and nobody was coming in now because of the downpour. It was pleasanter, they agreed, when there were enough candles burning before Sainte Anne to show the gold flowers on her cloak.

"Why don't you light a candle, Cécile?" Jacques asked. "You do, sometimes."

"Yes, but this morning I haven't any money with me."

Jacques sighed. "It would be nice," he repeated.

"I wonder, Jacques, if it would be wrong for me to take a candle, and then bring the ten sous down later, when the rain stops."

Jacques brightened. He thought that a very good idea.

"But it's irregular, Jacques. Perhaps it would not be right."

"You wouldn't forget, would you?"

"Oh, no! But I might be struck by lightning or something on the way home. And then, I expect, I'd die in sin."

66

"But I would tell your father, and he would give me the ten sous to put in the box. I wouldn't forget."

She saw he wanted very much to light a candle. "Well, perhaps. I'll try it this once, and I'll light one for you, too. Only be sure you don't forget, if anything happens to me."

They went softly up to the feet of Sainte Anne, where the candles were burning down in the metal basin. Each of them took a fresh taper from the box underneath, lit it, and fitted its hollow base upon one of the little metal horns. After saying a prayer they returned to their bench to enjoy the sight of the two new bright spots in the brownish gloom. Sure enough, when the fresh tapers were burning well, the gold flowers on Sainte Anne's cloak began to show; not entire, but wherever there was a fold in the mantle, the gold seemed to flow like a glistening liquid. Her figure emerged from the dusk in a rich, oily, yellow light.

After a long silence Jacques spoke.

"Cécile, all the saints in this church like children, don't they?"

"Oh, yes! And Our Lord loves children. Because He was a child Himself, you know."

Jacques had something else in mind. In a moment he brought it out. "Sometimes sailors are fond of children, too."

"Yes," she agreed with some hesitation.

He sensed a reservation in her voice.

"And they're awful brave," he went on feelingly. "If it wasn't for the sailors, we wouldn't have any ships from France, or anything."

"That's true," Cécile assented.

Jacques relapsed into silence. He was thinking of a jolly Breton sailor who had played with him in the summer, and carved him a marvellous beaver out of wood and painted its teeth white. He had sailed away on *La Garonne* three weeks ago, nearly breaking Jacques's heart. With that curious tact of childhood, which fails less often than the deepest diplomacy, Jacques almost never referred to his mother or her house or the people who came there, when he was with Cécile and her father. When he went to see them, he left his little past behind him, as it were.

At last the fall of water on the roof grew fainter, and the light clearer. Cécile said she must be going home now. "Come along with me, Jacques. Never mind about your clothes," seeing that he hung back, "that will be all right. Perhaps my father will give you a bath while I am getting our déjeuner, and we will all have our chocolate together."

As they quitted their bench, someone entered the church; a very heavy, tall old man with wide, stooping shoulders and a head hanging forward. When he took off his shovel hat at the door, a black skull-cap still remained over his scanty locks. He carried a cane and seemed to move his legs with some difficulty under his long, black gown. It was old Bishop Laval himself, who had been storm-bound for an hour and more at the house of one of the merchants on the square. Cécile hurried up to him before he should have time to kneel.

"Excuse me, Monseigneur l'Ancien," she said respectfully, "but if it is quite convenient would you be so kind as to lend me twenty sous?"

The old man looked down at her, frowning. His eyes were large and full, but set deep back under his forehead. He had such a very large, drooping nose, and such a grim, bitter mouth, that he might well have frightened a child who didn't know him. With considerable difficulty he got a little black purse out from under his gown. There was not much in it.

"You see," Cécile explained, "the little boy and I wished to offer candles, and I had no money with me. I was going up to my father's shop to get some, but I would rather not leave the church owing for the candles."

The old man nodded and looked slightly amused. He put two pieces in her hand, and she went to the front of the church to slip them in the box, leaving Jacques, who had got back against the wall as far as he could go, to bear the scrutiny of the Bishop's smouldering eyes. When she came back, she found them regarding each other in silence, but very intently; the old man staring down from his height, the little boy, his finger in his mouth, looking up at the Bishop shyly, but in a way that struck her as very personal. Cécile took him by the hand and led him to the door. Glancing back over her shoulder, she saw the Bishop sink heavily to his knees with something between a sigh and a groan.

Everything was glittering when they stepped out into the square; no sun yet, but a bright rain-grey light, silver and cut steel and pearl on the grey roofs and walls. Long veils of smoky fog were caught in the pine forests across the river. And how fresh the air smelled!

"Jacques," Cécile asked wonderingly, "do you know Monseigneur Laval? Did he ever talk to you?"

"I think once he did."

"What about?"

"I don't remember."

They went hand in hand up the hill.

He both did and did not remember; it came back to him in flashes, unrelated pictures, like a dream. Perhaps it was a dream. He could never have told Cécile about it, since it was hard for him to talk even about things he knew very well. But whenever he chanced to see old Bishop Laval, he felt that once, long ago, something pleasant had happened between them.

It had happened two years ago, when he was only four, before he knew the Auclairs at all. It was in January. A light, sticky snow had fallen irresolutely, at intervals, all day. Toward evening the weather changed; the sun emerged, just sinking over the great pine forest to the west, hung there, an angry ball, and all the snow-covered rock blazed in orange fire. The sun became a half-circle, then a mere red eyebrow, then dropped behind the forest, leaving the air clear blue, and much colder, with a pale lemon moon riding high overhead. There was no wind, it was a night of still moonlight, and within an hour after sunset the wet snow had frozen fast over roofs and spires and trees. Everything on the rock was sheathed in glittering white ice. It was a sight to stir the dullest blood. Some trappers from Three Rivers were in town. They had supper with La Grenouille, and afterwards persuaded her to go for a ride in their dog-sledges up the frozen St. Lawrence. Jacques was in bed asleep. 'Toinette threw an extra blanket over him and put an armful of wood in the stove, then went off with the young men, taking L'Escargot with her. She meant to be out only an hour or two; but they had plenty of brandy along to keep them warm, and so they made a night of it. Dog-sledging by moonlight on that broad marble highway, with no wind, was fine sport.

After she had been gone a couple of hours, Jacques wakened up very cold and called for his mother. Presently he got up and went to look for her. He went to L'Escargot's bed, and that, too, was empty. The moonlight shone in brightly, but the fire had gone out, and all about him things creaked with the cold. He found his shoes and an old shawl and went out into the snow to look for his mother. The poor neighbour houses were silent. He went behind the King's storehouse and up Notre Dame street to the market square. The worthy merchants were long ago in bed, and all the houses were dark except one, where the mother of the family was very sick. The statue of King Louis, with a cloak and helmet of snow, looked terrifying in the moonlight. Jacques already knew better than to knock at that solid, comfortable house where he saw a lighted window; he knew his mother wasn't well thought of by these rich people. Not knowing where to turn, he took the only forward way there was, up Mountain Hill.

Luckily, one other person was abroad that night. Old Bishop Laval, who never spared himself, had been down to the square to sit with the sick woman. He came toiling up the hill in his fur cloak and his tall fur cap, which was almost as imposing as his episcopal mitre, a cane in one hand, a lantern in the other. His valet followed behind. They were passing the new Bishop's Palace, now cold and empty, as Monseigneur de Saint-Vallier was in France. Just as they wound under the retaining wall of the terrace, they heard a child crying. The Bishop stopped and flashed his lantern this way and that. On the flight of stone steps that led up through the wall to the episcopal residence, he saw a little boy, almost a baby, sitting in the snow, crouching back against the masonry.

"Where does he belong?" asked the Bishop of his *donné*.

"Ah, that I cannot tell, Monseigneur," replied Houssart.

"Pick him up and bring him along," said the Bishop.

"Unbutton your coat and hold him against your body."
The lantern moved on.

The old Bishop lived in the Priests' House, built as
a part of his Seminary. His private rooms were poor
and small. All his silver plate and velvet and linen he had
given away little by little, to needy parishes, to needy
persons. He had given away the revenues of his abbeys
in France, and had transferred his vast grants of Canadian
land to the Seminary. He lived in naked poverty.

When they reached home, he commanded Houssart
to build a fire in the fireplace at once (had he been alone
he would have undressed and gone to bed in the cold)
and to heat water, that he might give the child a warm bath.

"Is there any milk?" he asked.

Houssart hesitated. "A little, for your chocolate in the
morning, Monseigneur."

"Get it and put it to warm on the hearth. Pour a little
cognac in it, and bring any bread there is in the house."

One strange thing Jacques could remember afterwards.
He was sitting on the edge of a narrow bed, wrapped in a
blanket, in the light of a blazing fire. He had just been
washed in warm water; the basin was still on the floor.
Beside it knelt a very large old man with big eyes and a
great drooping nose and a little black cap on his head,
and he was rubbing Jacques's feet and legs very softly
with a towel. They were all alone then, just the two of
them, and the fire was bright enough to see clearly. What
he remembered particularly was that this old man, after

he had dried him like this, bent down and took his foot in his hand and kissed it; first the one foot, then the other. That much Jacques remembered.

When the servant returned, they gave the child warm milk with a little bread in it, and put him into the Bishop's bed, though Houssart begged to take him to his own.

"No, we will not move him. He is falling asleep already. I do not know if that flush means a fever or not."

"Monseigneur," Houssart whispered, "now that I have seen him in the light, I recognize this child. He is the son of that 'Toinette Gaux, the woman they call La Grenouille."

"Ah!" the old man nodded thoughtfully. "That, too, may have a meaning. Throw more wood on the fire and go. I shall rest here in my arm-chair with my fur coat over my knees until it is time to ring the bell." The Bishop got up at four o'clock every morning, dressed without a fire, went with his lantern into the church, and rang the bell for early mass for the working people. Many good people who did not want to go to mass at all, when they heard that hoarse, frosty bell clanging out under the black sky where there was not yet even a hint of daybreak, groaned and went to the church. Because they thought of the old Bishop at the end of the bell-rope, and because his will was stronger than theirs. He was a stubborn, high-handed, tyrannical, quarrelsome old man, but no one could deny that he shepherded his sheep.

When his *donné* had gone and he was left with the

sleeping child, the Bishop settled his swollen legs upon a stool, covered them with his cloak, and sank into meditation. This was not an accident, he felt. Why had he found, on the steps of that costly episcopal residence built in scorn of him and his devotion to poverty, a male child, half-clad and crying in the merciless cold? Why had this reminder of his Infant Saviour been just there, under that house which he never passed without bitterness, which was like a thorn in his flesh? Had he been too much absorbed in his struggles with governors and intendants, in the heavy labour of founding and fixing his church upon this rock, in training a native priesthood and safeguarding their future?

Monseigneur de Laval had not always been a man of means and measures. Long ago, in Bernières's Hermitage at Caen, his life had been wholly given up to meditation and prayer. Not until he was sent out to Canada to convert a frontier mission into an enduring part of the Church had he become a man of action. His life, as he reviewed it, fell into two even periods. The first thirty-six years had been given to purely personal religion, to bringing his mind and will into subjection to his spiritual guides. The last thirty-six years had been spent in bringing the minds and wills of other people into subjection to his own,—since he had but one will, and that was the supremacy of the Church in Canada. Might this occurrence tonight be a sign that it was time to return to that rapt and mystical devotion of his earlier life?

In the morning, after he returned from offering early mass in the church, before it was yet light, the Bishop sent his man about over the hill, to this house and that, wherever there were young children, begging of one shoes, of another a little frock,—whatever the mother could spare from the backs of her own brood.

'Toinette Gaux had returned home meanwhile, and was frightened at missing her son. But she was ashamed to go out and look for him. Some neighbour would bring him back, she thought,—and, insolent as she was, she dreaded the moment. She got her deserts, certainly, when two long, black shadows fell upon the glistening snow before her door; the Bishop in his tall fur cap, prodding the icy crust with his cane, and behind him Houssart, carrying the little boy.

The Bishop came in without knocking, and motioned his man to put the child down and withdraw. He stood for some moments confronting the woman in silence. 'Toinette was no fool; she felt all his awfulness; the long line of noble blood and authority behind him, the power of the Church and the power of the man. She wished the earth would swallow her. Not a shred of her impudence was left her. Her tongue went dry. His silence was so dreadful that it was a relief when he began to thunder and tell her that even the beasts of the forest protected their young (*Les ourses et les louves protègent leurs petits*). He meant to watch over this boy, he said; if she neglected him, he would take the child and put him with

76

the Sisters of the Congregation, not here, but in Montreal, to place him as far as possible from a worthless mother.

'Toinette knew that he would do it, too. When she was a little girl, she used to hear talk about just such a high-handed proceeding of the Bishop's. A rich man in Quebec had brought a girl over from France to work as a bonne in his family. The Bishop thought she did not come to mass often enough and was not receiving proper religious training. So one day when he met her on the street, he took her by the hand and led her to the Ursuline convent and put her with the cloistered Sisters. There she stayed until the Governor gave her master a warrant to search the rock for his maid and take her wherever he found her. But 'Toinette knew that a woman of her sort, without money or good repute, had little chance of getting her boy back if once the Bishop took him away.

She kept Jacques in the house all the rest of the winter, and never went out herself except L'Escargot was there to watch him. It was not until the summer ships came, bringing new lovers and new distractions, that Jacques was allowed to go into the streets to play.

IV

Cécile was taking Jacques to Noël Pommier to be measured for his shoes. The cobbler lived half-way down Holy Family Hill, the steep street that plunged from the Cathedral down toward the St. Lawrence. There were other shoemakers in Quebec, but all persons of quality went to Pommier, unless they had had a short answer from him at some time. He would not hurry a piece of work for anybody,—not for the Count or the Intendant or the Bishop. If anyone tried to hurry him, he became surly and was likely to say something that a self-important person could not allow himself to overlook. It was rumoured that he had spoken unbecomingly to the valet of Monseigneur de Saint-Vallier, and had told him it would be better if his master had all his shoes made in Paris, where he spent so much of his time. Certainly the new Bishop had ceased to patronize him, which was a grief to Pommier's pious mother.

When the children entered the cobbler's door, they found him seated at his bench with a shoe between his knees, sewing the sole to the upper. Seeing that it was M. Auclair's daughter, he rose and put down his work. He was a thick-set man with stooped shoulders; his head was grown over with coarse black hair cut short like bristles, his fleshy face was dark red, and seamed with hard creases. The purple veins that spread like little roots about his nostrils suggested an occasional indulgence in brandy. When Pommier stood up, with his blackened hands hanging beside his leather apron, and his corded, hairy arms bare to the elbow, he looked like a black bear standing upright. His eyes, too, were small like a bear's, and somewhat bloodshot.

"Bonjour, Mademoiselle Cécile, what can I do for you?"

"If you please, Monsieur Pommier, I have brought little Jacques Gaux to be measured for his shoes. Has the Count's valet spoken to you about it?"

Pommier nodded. "Sit down there, little man, and let me see." He put Jacques down on a straw-topped stool (an old one his father had brought from Rouen, along with his bench and tools), took off the wretched foot-gear he had on, and began to study his feet and to make measurements.

While this was going on in deep silence, a door at the back of the house opened, and Pommier's mother, a thin, lively old woman with a crutch, came tapping lightly across the living-room and into the shop. She embraced Cécile with delight, and spoke very kindly to Jacques when he was presented to her.

"I have never seen this little fellow before, since I don't get about much, but I like to know all the children in Quebec. You will be very content with fine new shoes, my boy?"

"Oui, madame," Jacques murmured.

"And you have quite neglected me of late, Cécile. I know you are busy enough down there, but I have been looking for you every day since the ships sailed. My son saw your father at the market yesterday and observed that he was laying in good supplies for you." Madame Pommier seated herself on one of the wooden chairs without backs and rested her crutch across her knees. She always came into the shop when there were clients, and she liked to know what her son was doing every minute of the day.

When Cécile was little, Madame Pommier used to come to see her mother very often. She was one of the first friends Madame Auclair made in Quebec, and had given her a great deal of help in her struggle to keep house in a place where there were none of the conveniences to which she was accustomed. The Pommiers themselves were old residents, had lived here ever since this Noël was a young lad, and his father had been the Count's shoe-maker during his first governorship, twenty-odd years ago. Just about the time that Madame Auclair's health began to fail, Madame Pommier had fallen on the icy hill in front of her own door and broken her hip. The good chirurgien Gervaise Beaudoin attended her, but though the bone knit, it came together badly and left one leg much shorter than the other. M. Auclair had made a crutch for her, and as she was slight and very active, she was soon able to get about in her own house and attend to her duties. Many a time Cécile had found her by her stove, the crutch under her left arm, handling her pots and casseroles as deftly as if she were not propped up by a wooden stick. Sometimes in winter she even got to mass. Her son had set an arm-chair upon runners, and in this he pushed her up the hill over the snow to the Cathedral.

After the cobbler had made his measurements and noted them down, he took up his work again and began driving his awl through the leather, drawing the big needle with waxed thread through after it. Tools of any sort had a fascination for Cécile; she loved to watch a shoemaker or a carpenter at work. Jacques, who had never seen anything of the kind before, followed Pommier's black fingers with astonishment. They both sat quietly, and the old lady joined them in admiringly watching her clever son. Suddenly she bethought herself of something, and pointed with her crutch to a little cabinet of shelves covered by a curtain. There ladies' shoes, sent in for repair or made to order, were kept, as being rather too personal to expose on the open shelves with the men's boots.

"*Tirez, tirez,*" whispered Madame Pommier. Cécile got up and drew back the curtain, and at once knew what the old lady wished her to see: a beautiful pair of red satin slippers, embroidered in gold and purple, with leather soles and red leather heels.

"Oh, madame, how lovely! To whom do they belong?"

"To Monseigneur l'Ancien. They are his house slippers. My son is to put new soles on them,—see, they are almost worn through. Houssart says he paces his chamber in the night when he is at his devotions, so that he will not be overcome by sleep."

"But these are so small, can he possibly wear them? And his walk is so heavy, too."

"Ah, that is because of his legs, which are bad. But he has a very slender foot, very distinguished. That is the Montmorency in him; he is of noble blood, you know."

Here Pommier himself reached up to a row of wooden lasts over his head and handed one of them to Cécile.

"That is his foot, mademoiselle."

Cécile took the smoothly shaped wood in her hands and examined it curiously. On the sole Noël had scratched with his awl: "Mgr. Lav'."

"And next it," said Madame Pommier, "you will find the Governor's. He, too, has a fine foot, very high in the arch, but large, as is needful for a soldier. And there to the left is the Intendant's, and Madame de Champigny's."

"Oh, Monsieur Pommier, you have the feet of all the great people here! Did you make them all yourself?"

"Ah, no! Some are from my father's time. Yes, you may look at them if it amuses you."

Cécile took them down one after another. To be sure, they all looked a good deal alike to her, but she could guess the original of each form from the awl scratches on the sole. On one she spelled the letters "R. CAV." She was trying to think whose that might be, when Pommier startled her a little by saying in a very peculiar tone of voice:

"That foot will not come back."

She could not tell whether he was angry or sorry,— there was something so harsh in his tone.

"But why, Monsieur Noël, why not?"

"It went too far," he replied with the same bitter shortness.

She stared at the letters. The old lady beckoned her

and traced over the inscription with her finger. "That is my husband's marking; he always made capitals. It means Robert Cavelier de La Salle."

Cécile drew a deep breath. "Monsieur Noël believes he is really dead, then?"

Noël looked up from his black threads. "Everyone knows he is dead, mademoiselle. The people who say he will come back are fools. He was murdered, a thousand miles from here. Tonti brought the word. Robert de La Salle has come into this shop many a time when I was a lad. He was a true man, mademoiselle, and nobody was true to him, except Monsieur le Comte; not his own brother, nor his nephew, nor his King. It is always like that when there is a great one in a family. But I shall always keep his last. That foot went farther than any other in New France." He dropped his eyes and began driving his awl again.

Cécile knew it would be useless to question him,—such an outburst was most unusual from Pommier. But when she got home, she brought the matter up to her father and asked him whether it was true that the Abbé Cavelier had turned against his brother.

"I don't know, my dear. Nobody knows what happened down there. The Count blames him, but then, the Count always hated the Abbé."

V

It was the afternoon of All Saints' Day, and Jacques had come up the hill through a driving sleet storm to put on his new shoes for the first time. When he had carefully laced them, he stood up in them and, looking from one to the other of his friends, smiled a glad, surprised, soft smile. He was certainly not a handsome child, but he had one beauty,—his baby teeth. When his pale lips parted, his teeth showed like two rows of pearls, really; even, regular, all the same size, lustrous like those pearls that have just a faint shimmer of lilac. The hard crusts, which were his fare for the most part, kept them polished like veritable jewels. Cécile only hoped that when his second teeth came in, they would not be narrow and pointed, of the squirrel kind, like his mother's.

When M. Auclair asked Jacques if the shoes were comfortable, he looked up wonderingly and said: "Mais, oui, monsieur," as if they could not possibly be otherwise.

The apothecary went back into his shop, where he was boiling pine tops (*bourgeons des pins*) to make a cough-syrup. Cécile told Jacques she had found in her *Lives of the Saints* the picture of a little boy who looked very much like him.

"I shall always keep it for a picture of you, Jacques. Look, it is little Saint Edmond. He was an English saint, and he became Archbishop of Cantorbéry. But he died in France, at the monastery of Pontigny. Sit here beside me, and I will read you what it says about him.

"*Edmond était tout enfant un modèle de vertu, grâce aux tendres soins de sa pieuse mère. On ne le voyait qu'à l'école et à l'église, partageant ses journées entre la prière et l'étude, et se privant des plaisirs les plus innocents pour s'entretenir avec Jésus et sa divine Mère à laquelle il voua un culte tout spécial. Un jour qu'il fuyait ses compagnons de jeu, pour se recueillir intimement, l'Enfant Jésus lui apparaît, rayonnant de beauté et le regarde avec amour en lui disant: 'Je te salue, mon bien-aimé.' Edmond tout ébloui n'ose répondre et le divin Sauveur reprend: 'Vous ne me connaissez donc pas?—Non, avoue l'enfant, je n'ai pas cet honneur et je crois que vous ne devez pas me connaître non plus, mais me prenez pour un autre.—Comment, continue le petit Jésus, vous ne me reconnaissez pas, moi qui suis toujours à vos côtés et vous accompagne partout. Regardez-moi; je suis Jésus, gravez toujours ce nom en votre cœur et imprimez-le sur votre front et je vous préserverai de mort subite ainsi que tous ceux qui feront de même.'*"

The little woodcut in Cécile's old book showed the boy saint very like Jacques indeed; a clumsy little fellow, abashed at the apparition, standing awkwardly with his finger in his mouth; his chin had no tip, because the old block from which he was printed was worn away. Beside him stood the Heavenly Child, all surrounded by rays, just Edmond's height, friendly like a playfellow, and treading on the earth, not floating in the air as visions are wont to do. Jacques bent over the book, his thumb on the page to keep it flat, and asked Cécile to read it over again, so that he could remember. When she finished, he drew a long, happy sigh.

"I wish the little Jesus would appear to me like that, standing on the ground. Then I would not be frightened," he murmured.

"I don't believe He ever does, in Canada, Jacques. Though perhaps He appears to the recluse in Montreal, she is so very holy. I know angels come to her. But I expect He is often near you and keeps you from harm, as He said to Saint Edmond; *moi qui suis toujours à vos côtés et vous accompagne partout.* Now you can look at the other pictures while I make our chocolate. Since this is All Saints' Day, we ought to think a great deal about the saints."

Left in the corner of the red sofa, Jacques held the book, but he did not turn the pages. He sat looking at the logs burning in the fireplace and making gleams on the china shepherd boy, the object of his especial admiration. He heard the sleet pecking on the window-panes and thought how nice it was to have a place like this to come to. When the chocolate began to give off its rich odour, his nostrils quivered like a puppy's. Cécile carried her father's cup to him in the shop, and then she and Jacques sat down at one corner of the table, where she had spread a napkin over the cloth.

Much as Jacques loved chocolate (in so far as he knew,

this was the only house in the world in which that comforting drink was made), there was something he cared more about, something that gave him a kind of solemn satisfaction,—Cécile's cup. She had a silver cup with a handle; on the front was engraved a little wreath of roses, and inside that wreath was the name, "*Cécile*," cut in the silver. Her Aunt Clothilde had given it to her when she was but a tiny baby, so it had been hers all her life. That was what seemed so wonderful to Jacques. His clothes had always belonged to somebody else before they were made over for him; he slept wherever there was room for him, sometimes with his mother, sometimes on a bench. He had never had anything of his own except his toy beaver,—and now he would have his shoes, made just for him. But to have a little cup, with your name on it . . . even if you died, it would still be there, with your name.

More than the shop with all the white jars and mysterious implements, more than the carpet and curtains and the red sofa, that cup fixed Cécile as born to security and privileges. He regarded it with respectful, wistful admiration. Before the milk or chocolate was poured, he liked to hold it and trace with his finger-tips the letters that made it so peculiarly and almost sacredly hers. Since his attention was evidently fixed upon her cup, more than once Cécile had suggested that he drink his chocolate from it, and she would use another. But he shook his head, unable to explain. That was not at all what her cup meant to him. Indeed, Cécile could not know what it meant to him; she was too fortunate.

They had scarcely finished the last drop and the last crumb, when the shop door opened and they heard a woman's voice. Without a word Jacques slipped to the floor and began to take off his new shoes. Cécile sat still.

In the front shop Auclair was confronted by a vehement young woman, slightly out of breath, her head and shoulders tightly wrapped in a shawl, her cheeks reddened by the wind, and her fair hair curling about her forehead and glistening with water drops. The apothecary rose and said politely:

"Good day, 'Toinette, what will you have?"

She tossed her head. "None of your poisons, thank you! I believe my son is here?"

"I think so. He is in very good hands when he is here."

'Toinette struck an attitude, her hand on her hip. "Je suis mère, vous savez! The care of my son is my affair."

"Very true."

"What is this I hear about your getting shoes for him? I am his mother. I will get him shoes when I think it necessary. I am poor, it is true; but I want none of your money that is the price of poisons."

"Bien. I will take care that you get none of it. But I did not pay for the shoes. They were bought with the Governor's money."

'Toinette looked interested. Sharp points showed in her eyes, like the points of her teeth. "The Governor?

Ah, that is different. The Governor is our protector, he owes us something. And the King owes something to the children of those poor creatures, like my mother, whom he sent out here under false pretences."

Auclair held up a warning finger. He was sorry for her, because he saw how ill at ease she was under her impertinence. "Do not quarrel with the Government, my girl. That can do you no good, and it might get you into trouble."

'Toinette loosened her shawl and then wound it tight. She wished she had been more civil; perhaps they would have offered her some chocolate. She called shrilly for Jacques. He came at once, without saying a word, his new shoes in his hands, his old ones on his feet. His mother caught him by the shoulder with a jerk,—she could not cuff him in the apothecary's presence. "Au revoir, monsieur," she snapped, as Auclair opened the door for her. She went down the hill with her defiant stride, her head high, and Jacques walked after her as fast as he could, wearing an expression of intense gravity, blinking against the sleet, and carrying his new shoes, soles up, out in front of him in a most unnatural way, as if he were carrying a basin full of water and trying not to spill it.

Auclair thrust his head out and watched them round the turn, then closed the door. He looked in upon his daughter and remarked:

"She has shown her teeth; now she will not make any more trouble for a while. She will let him wear his shoes. She was pleased and was afraid of showing it."

"He pulled off his new stockings and stuffed them inside his shirt, Papa!"

Auclair laughed. "How often I have seen children and dogs, and even brave men, take on quick sly ways to protect themselves from an ill-tempered woman! I doubt whether she is very rough with him at home. When she is among people who look down on her, she takes it out on him."

That night after dinner they did not go for their usual walk, since the weather was so bleak, but sat by the fire listening to the rattle of the sleet on the windows.

"Papa," said Cécile, "shall you have a mass said for poor Bichet this year, as always?"

"Yes, on the tenth of November, the day on which he was hanged."

This mass Auclair had said at the Récollets' chapel where Count Frontenac heard mass every morning.

"Please tell me about Bichet again, and it will be fresh in my mind when I go to the mass."

"It will not keep you awake, as it did the first time I told you? We must not grieve about these things that happened long ago,—and this happened when the Count was in Canada the first time, while your grandfather and grandmother were both living.

"Poor old Bichet had lodged in our cellar since I was a boy. He was a knife-grinder and used to go out every day with his wheel on his back, and he picked up a few

sous at his trade. But he could never have kept himself
in shoes, having to walk so much, if your grandfather
had not given him his old ones. He paid us nothing for
his lodging, of course. He had his bed on the floor in a
dry corner of our cellar, where the sirops and elixirs
were kept. In very cold weather your grandmother would
put a couple of bricks among the coals when she was getting supper, and old Bichet would take these hot bricks
down and put them in his bed. And she often saved a cup
of hot soup and a piece of bread for the old man and let
him eat them in the warm kitchen, for he was very neat
and cleanly. When I had any spending-money, or when
I was given a fee for carrying medicines to some house in
the neighbourhood, I always saved a little for the old
knife-grinder. He was reserved and uncomplaining and
never inflicted his troubles upon us, though he must have
had many. On Saturdays, when your grandmother cooked
a joint and had a big fire, she used to heat a kettle of
water for him, and he carried it down to his corner and
washed himself. He was a Christian and went to mass.
He was a kind man, gentle to creatures below him,—
for there were those even worse off.

"Now, on the rue du Figuier stood a house that had
long been closed, for the family had gone to live at
Fontainebleau, and the empty coach-house was used as a
store-room for old pieces of furniture. The care-taker
was a careless fellow who went out to drink with his
cronies and left the place unguarded. In the coach-house

were two brass kettles which had lain there for many years, doing nobody any good. Bichet must have seen them often, as he went in and out to sharpen the caretaker's carving-knife.

"One night, when this fellow was carousing, Bichet carried off those two pots. He took them to an ironmonger and sold them. Nobody would ever have missed them; but Bichet had an enemy. Near us there lived a degenerate, half-witted boy of a cruel disposition. He tortured street cats, and even sparrows when he could catch them. Old Bichet had more than once caught him at his tricks and reproved him and set his victims at liberty. That boy was cunning, and he used to spy on Bichet. He saw him carrying off those brass kettles and reported him to the police. Bichet was seized in the street, when he was out with his grindstone, and taken to the Châtelet. He confessed at once and told where he had sold the pots. But that was not enough for the officers; they put him to torture and made him confess to a lifetime of crime; to having stolen from us and from the Frontenac house— which he had never done.

"Your grandfather and I hurried to the prison to speak for him. Your grandfather told them that a man so old and infirm would admit anything under fright and anguish, not knowing what he said; that a confession obtained under torture was not true evidence. This infuriated the Judge. If we would take oath that the prisoner had never stolen anything from us, they would put him into the strappado again and make him correct his confession. We saw that the only thing we could do for our old lodger was to let him pass quickly. Luckily for Bichet, the prison was overcrowded, and he was hanged the next morning.

"Your grandmother never got over it. She had for a long while struggled with asthma every winter, and that year when the asthma came on, she ceased to struggle. She said she had no wish to live longer in a world where such cruelties could happen."

"And I am like my grandmother," cried Cécile, catching her father's hand. "I do not want to live there. I had rather stay in Quebec always! Nobody is tortured here, except by the Indians, in the woods, and they know no better. But why does the King allow such things, when they tell us he is a kind King?"

"It is not the King, my dear, it is the Law. The Law is to protect property, and it thinks too much of property. A couple of brass pots, an old saddle, are reckoned worth more than a poor man's life. Christ would have forgiven Bichet, as He did the thief on the cross. We must think of him in paradise, where no law can touch him. I believe that harmless old man is in paradise long ago, and when I have a mass said for him every year, it is more for my own satisfaction than for his. I should like him to know, too, that our family remembers him."

"And I, Father, as long as I live, I will always have a mass said for Bichet on the day he died."

VI

On All Souls' Day Cécile went to church all day long; in the morning to the Ursuline chapel, in the afternoon to the Hôtel Dieu, and last of all down to the Church of Notre Dame de la Victoire to pray for her mother in the very spot where Madame Auclair had always knelt at mass. All the churches were full of sorrowful people; Cécile met them coming and going, and greeted them with lowered eyes and subdued voice, as was becoming. But she herself was not sorrowful, though she supposed she was.

The devotions of the day had begun an hour after midnight. Old Bishop Laval had no thought that anyone should forget the solemn duties of the time. He was at his post at one o'clock in the morning to ring the Cathedral bell, and from then on until early mass he rang it every hour. It called out through the intense silence of streets where there were no vehicles to rumble, but only damp vapours from the river to make sound more intense and startling, to give it overtones and singular reverberations.

> *"Priez pour les Morts,*
> *Vous qui reposez,*
> *Priez pour les tré-pas-sés!"*

it seemed to say, as if the exacting old priest himself were calling. One had scarcely time to murmur a prayer and turn over in one's warm bed, before the bell rang out again.

At twelve years it is impossible to be sad on holy days, even on a day of sorrow; at that age the dark things, death, bereavement, suffering, have only a dramatic value, —seem but strong and moving colours in the grey stretch of time.

On such solemn days all the stories of the rock came to life for Cécile; the shades of the early martyrs and great missionaries drew close about her. All the miracles that had happened there, and the dreams that had been dreamed, came out of the fog; every spire, every ledge and pinnacle, took on the splendour of legend. When one passed by the Jesuits', those solid walls seemed sentinelled by a glorious company of martyrs, martyrs who were explorers and heroes as well; at the Hôtel Dieu, Mother Catherine de Saint-Augustin and her story rose up before one; at the Ursulines', Marie de l'Incarnation overshadowed the living.

At Notre Dame de la Victoire one remembered the miraculous preservation for which it had been named, when this little church, with the banner of the Virgin floating from its steeple, had stood untouched through Sir William Phips's bombardment, though every heretic gun was aimed at it. Cécile herself could remember that time very well; the Lower Town had been abandoned, and she and her mother, with the other women and children, were hidden in the cellars of the Ursuline convent.

Even there they were not out of gun range; a shell had fallen into the court just as Sister Agatha was crossing it, and had taken off the skirt of her apron, though the Sister herself was not harmed.

To the older people of Kebec, All Souls' was a day of sad remembrance. Their minds went back to churches and cemeteries far away. Now the long closed season was upon them, and there would be no letters, no word of any kind from France for seven, perhaps eight, months. The last letters that came in the autumn always brought disturbing news to one household or another; word that a mother was failing, that a son had been wounded in the wars, that a sister had gone into a decline. Friends at home seemed to forget how the Canadians would have these gloomy tidings to brood upon all the long winter and the long spring, so that many a man and woman dreaded the arrival of those longed-for summer ships.

Fears for the sick and old so far away, sorrow for those who died last year—five years ago—many years ago,—memories of families once together and now scattered; these things hung over the rock of Kebec on this day of the dead like the dark fogs from the river. The cheerful faces were those in the convents. The Ursulines and the Hospitalières, indeed, were scarcely exiles. When they came across the Atlantic, they brought their family with them, their kindred, their closest friends. In whatever little wooden vessel they had laboured across the sea, they carried all; they brought to Canada the Holy Family, the saints and martyrs, the glorious company of the Apostles, the heavenly host.

Courageous these Sisters were, accepting good and ill fortune with high spirit,—with humour, even. They never vulgarly exaggerated hardships and dangers. They had no hours of nostalgia, for they were quite as near the realities of their lives in Quebec as in Dieppe or Tours. They were still in their accustomed place in the world of the mind (which for each of us is the only world), and they had the same well-ordered universe about them: this all-important earth, created by God for a great purpose, the sun which He made to light it by day, the moon which He made to light it by night,—and the stars, made to beautify the vault of heaven like frescoes, and to be a clock and compass for man. And in this safe, lovingly arranged and ordered universe (not too vast, though nobly spacious), in this congenial universe, the drama of man went on at Quebec just as at home, and the Sisters played their accustomed part in it. There was sin, of course, and there was punishment after death; but there was always hope, even for the most depraved; and for those who died repentant, the Sisters' prayers could do much,—no one might say how much.

So the nuns, those who were cloistered and those who came and went about the town, were always cheerful, never lugubrious. Their voices, even when they spoke to one through the veiled grille, were pleasant and inspiriting to hear. Most of them spoke good French, some the exquisite French of Tours. They conversed blithely, elegantly. When, on parting from a stranger, a Sister said pleasantly: "I hope we shall meet in heaven," that meant nothing doleful,—it meant a happy appointment, for tomorrow, perhaps!

Inferretque deos Latio. When an adventurer carries his gods with him into a remote and savage country, the colony he founds will, from the beginning, have graces, traditions, riches of the mind and spirit. Its history will shine with bright incidents, slight, perhaps, but precious, as in life itself, where the great matters are often as worthless as astronomical distances, and the trifles dear as the heart's blood.

VII

A heavy snowfall in December meant that winter had come,—the deepest reality of Canadian life. The snow fell all through the night of St. Nicholas' Day, but morning broke brilliant and clear, without a wisp of fog, and when one stepped out of the door, the sunlight on the glittering terraces of rock was almost too intense to be borne; one closed one's eyes and seemed to swim in throbbing red. Before noon there was a little thaw, the snow grew soft on top. But as the day wore on, a cold wind came up and the surface froze, to the great delight of the children of Quebec. By three o'clock a crowd of them were coasting down the steep hill named for the

Holy Family, among them Cécile and her protégé. Before she and her father had finished their déjeuner, Jacques had appeared at the shop door, wearing an expectant, hopeful look unusual to him. Cécile remembered that she had promised to take him coasting on her sled when the first snow came. She unfastened his ragged jacket and buttoned him into an old fur coat that she had long ago outgrown. Her mother had put it away in one of the chests upstairs, not because she expected ever to have another child, but because all serviceable things deserve to be taken care of.

When they reached the coasting-hill, the sun was already well down the western sky (it would set by four o'clock), and the light on the snow was more orange than golden; the long, steep street and the little houses on either side were a cold blue, washed over with rose-colour. They went down double,—Jacques sat in front, and Cécile, after she had given the sled a running start, dropped on the board behind him. Every time they reached the bottom, they trudged back up the hill to the front of the Cathedral, where the street began.

When the sun had almost sunk behind the black ridges of the western forest, Cécile and Jacques sat down on the Cathedral steps to eat their goûter. While they sat there, the other children began to go home, and the air grew colder. Now they had the hill all to themselves,—and this was the most beautiful part of the afternoon. They thought they would like to go down once more. With a quick push-off their sled shot down through constantly changing colour; deeper and deeper into violet, blue, purple, until at the bottom it was almost black. As they climbed up again, they watched the last flames of orange light burn off the high points of the rock. The slender spire of the Récollet chapel, up by the Château, held the gleam longest of all.

Cécile saw that Jacques was cold. They were not far from Noël Pommier's door, so she said they would go in and get warm.

The cobbler had pulled his bench close to the window and was making the most of the last daylight. Cécile begged him not to get up.

"We have only come in to get warm, Monsieur Pommier."

"Very good. You know the way. Come here, my boy, let me see whether your shoes keep the snow out." He reached for Jacques's foot, felt the leather, and nodded. Cécile passed into the room behind the shop, called to Madame Pommier in her kitchen, and asked if they might sit by her fire.

"Certainly, my dear, find a chair. And little Jacques may have my footstool; it is just big enough for him. Noël," she called, "come put some wood on the fire, these children are frozen." She came in bringing two squares of maple sugar—and a towel for Jacques to wipe his fingers on. He took the sugar and thanked her, but she saw that his eyes were fixed upon a dark corner of the room where a little copper lamp was burning before some coloured pictures. "That is my chapel, Jacques. You see, being lame, I do not get to mass very often, so I have a little chapel of my own, and the lamp burns night and day, like the sanctuary lamp. There is the Holy Mother and Child, and Saint Joseph, and on the other side are Sainte Anne and Saint Joachim. I am especially devoted to the Holy Family."

Drawn out by something in her voice, Jacques ventured a question.

"Is that why this is called Holy Family Hill, madame?"

Madame Pommier laughed and stooped to pat his head. "Quite the other way about, my boy! I insisted upon living here because the hill bore that name. My husband was for settling in the Basse Ville, thinking it would be better for his trade. But we have not starved here; those for whom the street was named have looked out for us, maybe. When we first came to this country, I was especially struck by the veneration in which the Holy Family was held in Kebec, and I found it was so all out through the distant parishes. I never knew its like at home. Monseigneur Laval himself has told me that there is no other place in the world where the people are so devoted to the Holy Family as here in our own Canada. It is something very special to us."

Cécile liked to think they had things of their own in Canada. The martyrdoms of the early Church which she read about in her *Lives of the Saints* never seemed to her half so wonderful or so terrible as the martyrdoms of

Father Brébeuf, Father Lalemant, Father Jogues, and their intrepid companions. To be thrown into the Rhone or the Moselle, to be decapitated at Lyon,—what was that to the tortures the Jesuit missionaries endured at the hands of the Iroquois, in those savage, interminable forests? And could the devotion of Sainte Geneviève or Sainte Philomène be compared to that of Mother Catherine de Saint-Augustin or Mother Marie de l'Incarnation?

"My child, I believe you are sleepy," said Madame Pommier presently, when both her visitors had been silent a long while. She liked her friends to be entertaining.

Cécile started out of her reverie. "No, madame, but I was thinking of a surprise I have at home, and perhaps I had better tell you about it now. You remember my Aunt Clothilde? I am sure my mother often talked to you of her. Last summer she sent me a box on *La Licorne:* a large wooden box, with a letter telling me not to open it. We must not open it until the day before Christmas, because it is a crèche; so, you see, we shall have a Holy Family, too. And we have been hoping that on Christmas Eve, before the midnight mass, Monsieur Noël will bring you to see it. You have not been in our house, you know, since my mother died."

"Noël, my son, what do you say to that?"

The cobbler had come in from the shop to light his candle at the fire.

"The invitation is for you too, Monsieur Noël, from my father."

The cobbler smiled and stood with the stump of candle in his hand before bending down to the blaze.

"That can be managed, and my thanks to monsieur your father. If there is snow, I will push my mother down in her sledge, and if the ground is naked, I will carry her on my back. She is no great weight."

"I shall like to see the inside of your house again, Cécile. I miss it. I have not been there since that time when your mother was ill, and Madame de Champigny sent her carriage to convey me."

Cécile remembered the time very well. It was after old Madame Pommier was crippled; Madame Auclair had long been too ill to leave the house. There was then only one closed carriage in Quebec, and that belonged to Madame de Champigny, wife of the Intendant. In some way she heard that the apothecary's sick wife longed to see her old friend, and she sent her *carrosse* to take Madame Pommier to the Auclairs'. It was a mark of the respect in which the cobbler and his mother were held in the community.

When Jacques and Cécile ran out into the cold again, from the houses along the tilted street the evening candle-light was already shining softly. Up at the top of the hill, behind the Cathedral, that second afterglow, which often happens in Quebec, had come on more glorious than the first. All the western sky, which had been hard and clear when the sun sank, was now throbbing with fiery vapours, like rapids of clouds; and between, the sky shone with a blue to ravish the heart,—that limpid, celestial, holy blue that is only seen when the light is golden.

"Are you tired, Jacques?"

"A little, my legs are," he admitted.

"Get on the sled and I will pull you up. See, there's the evening star—how near it looks! Jacques, don't you love winter?" She put the sled-rope under her arms, gave her weight to it, and began to climb. A feeling came over her that there would never be anything better in the world for her than this; to be pulling Jacques on her sled, with the tender, burning sky before her, and on each side, in the dusk, the kindly lights from neighbours' houses. If the Count should go back with the ships next summer, and her father with him, how could she bear it, she wondered. On a foreign shore, in a foreign city (yes, for her a foreign shore), would not her heart break for just this? For this rock and this winter, this feeling of being in one's own place, for the soft content of pulling Jacques up Holy Family Hill into paler and paler levels of blue air, like a diver coming up from the deep sea.

VIII

On the morning of the twenty-fourth of December Cécile lay snug in her trundle-bed, while her father lit the fires and prepared the chocolate. Although the heavy red curtains had not yet been drawn back, she knew that it was snowing; she had heard the crunch of fresh snow under the Pigeon boy's feet when he brought the morning loaf to the kitchen door. Even before that, when the bell rang for five o'clock mass, she knew by its heavy, muffled tone that the air was thick with snow and that it was not very cold. Whenever she heard the early bell, it was as if she could see the old Bishop with his lantern at the end of the bell-rope, and the cold of the church up there made her own bed seem the warmer and softer. In winter the old man usually carried a little basin as well as his lantern. It was his custom to take the bowl of holy water from the font in the evening, carry it into his kitchen, and put it on the back of the stove, where enough warmth would linger through the night to keep it from freezing. Then, in the morning, those who came to early mass would not have a mere lump of ice to peck at. Monseigneur de Laval was very particular about the consecrated oils and the holy water; it was not enough for him that people should merely go through the forms.

Cécile did not always waken at the first bell, which rang in the coldest hour of the night, but when she did, she felt a peculiar sense of security, as if there must be powerful protection for Kebec in such steadfastness, and the new day, which was yet darkness, was beginning as it should. The punctual bell and the stern old Bishop who rang it began an orderly procession of activities and held life together on the rock, though the winds lashed it and the billows of snow drove over it.

With the sound of the crackling fire a cool, mysterious fragrance of the forest, very exciting because it was under a roof, came in from the kitchen,—the breath of all the fir boughs and green moss that Cécile and Blinker had brought in yesterday from the Jesuits' wood. Today they would unpack the crèche from France,—the box that had come on *La Licorne* in midsummer and had lain upstairs unopened for all these months.

Auclair brought the chocolate and placed it on a little table beside his daughter's bed. They always breakfasted like this in winter, while the house was getting warm. This morning they had finally to decide where they would set out the crèche. Weeks ago they had agreed to arrange it in the deep window behind the sofa,—but then the sofa would have to be put on the other side of the room! This morning they found the thought of moving the sofa, where Madame Auclair used so often to recline, unendurable. It would quite destroy the harmony of their salon. The room, the house indeed, seemed to cling about that sofa as a centre.

There was another window in the room,—seldom uncurtained, because it opened directly upon the side wall of the baker's house, and the outlook was uninteresting. It was narrow, but Auclair said he could remedy that. As soon as his shop was put in order, he would construct a shelf in front of the window-sill, but a little lower; then the scene could be arranged in two terraces, as was customary at home.

Cécile spent the morning covering the window and the new shelf with moss and fir branches until it looked like a corner in the forest, and at noon she waylaid Blinker, just getting up from his bed behind the baker's ovens, and sent him to go and hunt for Jacques.

When Blinker returned with the boy, he himself looked in through the door so wistfully that Cécile asked him to come and open the box for her in the kitchen. There were a great number of little figures in the crate, each wrapped in a sheath of straw. As Blinker took them one at a time out of the straw and handed them to Cécile, he kept exclaiming: "Regardez, ma'm'selle, un beau petit âne!" . . . "Voilà, le beau mouton!" Cécile had never seen him come so far out of his shell; she had supposed that his shrinking sullenness was a part of him, like his crooked eyes or his red hair. When all the figures were unwrapped and placed on the dining-table in the salon, Blinker gathered up the straw and carried it with the crate into the cellar. She had thought that would be the last of him, but when he came back and stood again in the doorway, she hadn't the heart to send him away. She asked him to come in and sit down by the fire. Her mother had never done that, but today there seemed no way out of it. The fête which she meant so especially for Jacques, turned out to be even more for Blinker.

Jacques, indeed, was so bewildered as to seem apathetic, and was afraid to touch anything. Only when Cécile directed him would he take up one of the figures from the table and carry it carefully to the window where she was making the scene. The Holy Family must be placed first, under a little booth of fir branches. The Infant was not in His Mother's arms, of course, but lay rosy and naked in a little straw-lined manger, in which he had crossed the ocean. The Blessed Virgin wore no halo, but a white scarf over her head. She looked like a country girl, very naïve, seated on a stool, with her knees well apart under her full skirt, and very large feet. Saint Joseph, a grave old man in brown, with a bald head and wrinkled brow, was placed opposite her, and the ox and the ass before the manger.

"Those are all that go inside the stable," Cécile explained, "except the two angels. We must put them behind the manger; they are still watching over Him."

"Is that the stable, Cécile? I think it's too pretty for a stable," Jacques observed.

"It's a little *cabine* of branches, like those the first missionaries built down by Notre Dame des Anges, when they landed here long ago. They used to say the mass in a little shelter like that, made of green fir boughs."

Jacques touched one of the unassorted figures on the table with the tip of his finger. "Cécile, what are those animals?"

"Why, those are the camels, Jacques. Did you never see pictures of them? The three Kings came on camels, because they can go a long time without water and carry heavy loads. They carried the gold and frankincense and myrrh."

"I don't think I know about the Kings and the Shepherds very well," Jacques sighed. "I wish you would tell me."

While she placed the figures, Cécile began the story, and Jacques listened as if he had never heard it before. There was another listener, by the fireplace behind her, and she had entirely forgotten him until, with a sniffling sound, Blinker suddenly got up and went out through the kitchen, wiping his nose on his sleeve. Then Jacques noticed how dusky it had grown in the room; the window behind the sofa was a square of dull grey, like a hole in the wall of the house. He caught up his cap and ran out through the shop, calling back: "Oh, I am late!"

Jacques had been gone only a few minutes when Giorgio, the drummer boy from the Château, came in to see the crèche, and to bid Cécile good-bye for three days, as the Count had let him off to go home to his family on the Île d'Orléans. He had left his drum in the guard-house, and already he felt free. He would walk the seven miles up to Montmorency (perhaps he would be lucky enough to catch a ride in some farmer's sledge for part of the way), then cross the river on the ice. The north channel had been frozen hard for several weeks now. He would have a long walk after he got over to the island, too; but even if the night were dark, he knew the way, and he would get there in time to hear mass at his own paroisse. After mass his family would make réveillon,—music and dancing, and a supper with blood sausages and pickled pigs' feet and dainties of that sort.

"And before daybreak, mademoiselle, my grandfather will play the Alpine horn. He always does that on Christmas morning. If you were awake, you would hear it even over here. Such a beautiful sound it has, and the old man plays so true!"

Georges bought some cloves and bay-leaves for his mother (he had just been paid, and rattled the coins in his pocket), then started up the hill with such a happy face that Cécile wished she were going with him, over those seven snowy miles to Montmorency.

"He will almost certainly catch a ride," her father told her. "Even on the river there will be sledges coming and going tonight."

IX

That evening, soon after the dinner-table was cleared, the Auclairs heard a rapping at the shop door and went out to receive Madame Pommier in her chair on runners, very like the sledges in which great ladies used to travel at home. Her son lifted her out in all her wrappings and carried her into the salon, where the apothecary's armchair was set for her. But before she would accept this seat of honour, she must hobble all over the house to satisfy herself that things were kept just as they used to be in Madame Auclair's time. She found everything the same, she said, even to Blinker, having his sip of brandy in the kitchen.

After they had settled down before the fire to wait for

the Pigeons, who were always late, Jacques Gaux came hurrying in through the shop, looking determined and excited. He forgot to speak to the visitors and went straight up to Cécile, holding out something wrapped in a twist of paper, such as the merchants used for small purchases.

"I have a surprise for you," he said. "It is for the crèche, for the little Jesus."

When she took off the paper, she held in her hand Jacques's well-known beaver.

"Oh, Jacques, how nice of you! I don't believe there was ever a beaver in a crèche before." She was a little perplexed; the animal was so untraditional—what was she to do with him?

"He isn't new," Jacques went on anxiously. "He's just my little old beaver the sailor made me, but he could keep the baby warm. I take him to bed with me when I'm cold sometimes, and he keeps me warm."

Madame Pommier's sharp ears had overheard this conversation, and she touched Cécile with the end of her crutch. "Certainly, my dear, put it there with the lambs, before the manger. Our Lord died for Canada as well as for the world over there, and the beaver is our very special animal."

Immediately Madame Pigeon and her six children arrived. Auclair brought out his best liqueurs, and the Pommiers and Pigeons, being from the same parish in Rouen, began recalling old friends at home. Cécile was kept busy filling little glasses, but she noticed that Jacques was content, standing beside the crèche like a sentinel, paying no heed to the Pigeon children or anyone else, quite lost in the satisfaction of seeing his beaver placed in a scene so radiant. Before the evening was half over, he started up suddenly and began looking for his coat and cap. Cécile followed him into the shop.

"Don't you want your beaver, Jacques? Or will you leave him until Epiphany?"

He looked up at her, astonished, a little hurt, and quickly thrust his hands behind him. "Non, c'est pour toujours," he said decisively, and went out of the door.

"See, madame," Madame Pommier was whispering to Madame Pigeon, "we have a bad woman amongst us, and one of her clients makes a toy for her son, and he gives it to the Holy Child for a birthday present. That is very nice."

"C'est ça, madame, c'est ça," said matter-of-fact Madame Pigeon, quite liking the idea, now that her attention was called to it.

By eleven o'clock the company had become a little heavy from the heat of the fire and the good wine from the Count's cellar, and everyone felt a need of the crisp out-of-doors air. The weather had changed at noon, and now the stars were flashing in a clear sky,—a sky almost over-jewelled on that glorious night. The three families agreed that it would be well to start for the church very early and get good places. The Cathedral would be full to the doors tonight. Monseigneur de Saint-Vallier was to say the mass, and the old Bishop would be present, with a great number of clergy, and the Seminarians were to sing the music. Monseigneur de Saint-Vallier would doubtless wear the aube of rich lace given him by Madame de Maintenon for his consecration at Saint-Sulpice, in Paris, ten years ago. In one matter he and the old Bishop always agreed; that the services of the Church should be performed in Quebec as elaborately, as splendidly, as anywhere else in the world. For many years Bishop Laval had kept himself miserably poor to make the altar and the sacristy rich.

After everyone had had a last glass of liqueur, Madame Pommier was carried out to her sledge and tucked under her bearskin. The company proceeded slowly; pushing the chair up the steep curves of Mountain Hill and around the Récollet chapel, over fresh snow that had not packed, was a little difficult. When they reached the top of the rock, many houses were alight. Across the white ledges that sloped like a vast natural stairway down to the Cathedral, black groups were moving, families and friends in little flocks, all going toward the same goal,—the doors of the church, wide open and showing a ruddy vault in the blue darkness.

BOOK III
THE LONG WINTER

THE LONG WINTER

I

One morning between Christmas and New Year's Day a man still young, of a handsome but unstable countenance, clad in a black cassock with violet piping, and a rich fur mantle, entered the apothecary shop, greeted the proprietor politely, and asked for four boxes of sugared lemon peel.

It was not the young Bishop's custom to do his shopping himself; he sent his valet. This was the first time he had ever come inside the pharmacy. Auclair took off his apron as a mark of respect to a distinguished visitor, but replied firmly that, much to his regret, he had only three boxes left, and one of them he meant to send as a New Year's greeting to Mother Juschereau, at the Hôtel Dieu. He would be happy to supply Monseigneur de Saint-Vallier with the other two; and he had several boxes of apricots put down in sugar, if they would be of any use to him. Monseigneur declared they would do very well, paid for them, and said he would carry them away himself. Auclair protested that he or his little daughter could leave them at the Palace. But no, the Bishop insisted upon carrying his parcel. As he did not leave the shop at once, Auclair begged him to be seated.

Saint-Vallier sat down and threw back his fur mantle. "Have you by any chance seen Monseigneur de Laval of late?" he inquired. "I am deeply concerned about his health."

"No, Monseigneur, I have not seen him since the mass on Christmas Eve. But the bell has been ringing every morning as usual."

Saint-Vallier's arched eyebrows rose still higher, and he made a graceful, conciliatory gesture with his hand. "Ah, his habits, you know; one cannot interfere with them! But his valet told mine that the ulcer on his master's leg had broken out again, and that seems to me dangerous."

"I am sorry to hear it," said Auclair. "It is hardly dangerous, but painful and distressing."

"Especially so, since he will not remain in bed, and conceals the extent of his suffering even from his own Seminarians." The Bishop paused a moment, then continued in a tone so confidential as to be flattering. "I have been wondering, Monsieur Auclair, whether, provided we could obtain his consent, you would be willing to try a cauterization of the arm, to draw the inflammation away from the affected part. This was done with great success for Père La Chaise, the King's confessor, who had an ulcer between the toes while I was in office at Versailles."

"That was probably a form of gout," Auclair observed. "Monseigneur de Laval's affliction is quite different. He suffers from enlarged and congested veins in the leg. Such ulcers are hard to heal, but they are seldom fatal."

"But why not at least try the simple remedy which was so beneficial in the case of Père La Chaise?" urged the Bishop. There was a shallow brilliance in his large fine eyes which made Auclair antagonistic.

"Because, Monseigneur," he said firmly, "I do not believe in it; and because it has been tried already. Two years ago, when you were in France, Doctor Beaudoin made a cauterization upon Monseigneur de Laval, and he has since told me that he believes it was useless."

The Bishop looked thoughtfully about at the white jars on the shelves. "You are very advanced in your theories of medicine, are you not, Monsieur Auclair?"

"On the contrary, I am very old-fashioned. I think the methods of the last century better than those of the present time."

"Then you do not believe in progress?"

"Change is not always progress, Monseigneur." Auclair spoke quietly, but there was meaning in his tone. Saint-Vallier made some polite inquiry about the condition of old Doctor Beaudoin, and took his leave. His call,

Auclair suspected, was one of the overtures he occasionally made to people who were known partisans of old
Bishop Laval.

During the stay in France from which he had lately
returned, Monseigneur de Saint-Vallier had induced the
King to reverse entirely Laval's system for the training
and government of the Canadian clergy, thus defeating the
dearest wishes of the old man's heart and undoing the devoted labour of twenty years. Everything that made Laval's
Seminary unique and specially fitted to the needs of the
colony had been wiped out. His system of a movable
clergy, sent hither and thither out among the parishes at
the Bishop's discretion and always returning to the Seminary as their head and centre, had been changed by royal
edict to the plan of appointing curés to permanent liv-
ings, as in France,—a method ill fitted to a new, wild
country where within a year the population of any parish
might be reduced by half. The Seminary, which Laval
had made a thing of power and the centre of ecclesiastical
authority, a chapter, almost an independent order, was
now reduced to the state of a small school for training
young men for the priesthood.

These were some of the griefs that made the old
Bishop bear so mournful a countenance. The wilfulness
of his successor (chosen by himself, he must always bitterly remember!) went even further; Saint-Vallier had
taken away books and vases and furniture from the Seminary to enrich his new Palace. It was whispered that he

had made his Palace so large because he intended to take away the old Bishop's Seminarians and transfer them to the episcopal residence, to have them under his own eye. If this were done, Bishop Laval would be left living in the Priests' House, guarding a lofty building of long, echoing corridors and empty dormitories, round a deserted courtyard where the grass would soon be growing between the stones. Monseigneur Laval's friends could but hope that de Saint-Vallier would be off for France again before he carried out this threat.

Saint-Vallier was a man of contradictions, and they were stamped upon his face. One saw there something slightly hysterical, and something uncertain,—though his manner was imperious, and his administration had been arrogant and despotic. Auclair had once remarked to the Count that the new Bishop looked less like a churchman than like a courtier. "Or an actor," the Count replied with a shrug. Large almond-shaped eyes under low-growing brown hair and delicate eyebrows, a long, sharp nose—and then the lower part of his face diminished, like the neck of a pear. His mouth was large and well shaped, but seldom in repose; his chin narrow, receding, with a dimple at the end. He had a dark skin and flashing white teeth like an Italian,—indeed, his face recalled the portraits of eccentric Florentine nobles. He was still only forty-four; he had been Bishop of Quebec now twelve years,—and seven of them had been spent in France!

Auclair had never liked de Saint-Vallier. He did not doubt the young Bishop's piety, but he very much doubted his judgment. He was rash and precipitate, he was volatile. He acted too often without counting the cost, from some dazzling conception,—one could not say from impulse, for impulses are from the heart. He liked to reorganize and change things for the sake of change, to make a fine gesture. He destroyed the old before he had clearly thought out the new. When he first came to Canada, he won all hearts by his splendid charities; but he went back to France leaving the Seminary many thousand francs in debt as the result of his generous disbursements, and the old Bishop had to pay this debt out of the Seminary revenues. For years now, he had seemed feverishly determined to undo whatever he could of the old Bishop's work. This was the more galling to the old man because he himself had gone to France and chosen de Saint-Vallier and recommended him to Rome. Saint-Vallier had at first exhibited the most delicate consideration for his aged predecessor, but this attitude lasted only a short while. He was as changeable and fickle as a woman. Indeed, he had received a large part of his training under a woman, though by no means a fickle or capricious one.

When Jean Baptiste de la Croix de Chevrières de Saint-Vallier came to Court in the capacity of the King's almoner, Madame de Maintenon was past the age of youthful folly, —if indeed she had ever known such an age. (A poor girl from the West Indies, landing penniless in France with all her possessions in a band-box, she had had little time for follies, except such as helped her to get on in the world.) The young priest who was one day to be the second Bishop of Quebec knew her only after she had become the grave and far-seeing woman who so greatly influenced the King for the last thirty years of his reign.

Saint-Vallier was the seventh child of a noble family of Dauphiné. His eldest brother, Comte de Saint-Vallier, was Captain of the King's Guard, and secured for the young priest the appointment of *Aumônier ordinaire* to the King when he was but twenty-three years of age. He retained that office for nearly ten years, and was constantly in accord with Madame de Maintenon in emptying the King's purse for worthy charities. Saint-Vallier was by no means without enemies at Court. The clergy and even the Archbishop of Paris disliked him. They considered that he made his piety too conspicuous and was lacking in good taste. His oval face, with the bloom of youth upon it, his beautiful eyes, full of humility and scorn at the same time, were seen too much and too often. He had a hundred ways of making himself stand out from the throng, and his exceptional piety was like a reproach to those of the clergy who were more conventional and perhaps more worldly. He obtained from the King special permission to wear at Court the long black gown, which at that time was not worn by the priests at Versailles. So attired, he was more conspicuous than courtiers the most richly apparelled. His fellow abbés found de Saint-Vallier's acts of humility undignified, and his brother, the Captain of the Guard, found them ridiculous. One day the Captain met the Abbé following the Sacrament through the street, ringing a little hand-bell. The Captain awaited his brother's return to the Palace and told him angrily that his conduct was unworthy of his family, and that he had better retire to La Trappe, where his piety would be without an audience. But to be without an audience was the last thing the young Abbé desired.

Nevertheless, in his own way he was a sincere man. He refused the rich and honourable bishopric of Tours, repeatedly offered him by the King, and accepted the bishopric of Quebec,—the poorest and most comfortless honour the Crown had to offer.

By the time de Saint-Vallier made his third trip back to France, the King knew very well that he was not much wanted in Canada; every boat brought complaints of his arrogance and his rash impracticality. The King could not unmake a bishop, once he was consecrated, but he could detain him in France,—and that he did, for three years. During de Saint-Vallier's long absences in Europe his duties devolved upon Monseigneur de Laval. There was no one else in Canada who could ordain priests, administer the sacrament of confirmation, consecrate the holy oils. Though in the performance of these duties the old Bishop had to make long journeys in canoes and sledges, very fatiguing at his age, he undertook them without a murmur. He was glad to take up again the burdens he had once so gladly laid down.

II

After Epiphany, Auclair was away from home a great deal. The old chirurgien Gervaise Beaudoin was ill, and the apothecary went to see him every afternoon, leaving Cécile to tend the shop. When he was at home, he was much occupied in making cough-syrups from pine tops, and from horehound and honey with a little laudanum; or he was compounding tonics, and liniments for rheumatism. The months that were dull for the merchants were the busiest for him. He and his daughter seldom went abroad together now, but their weekly visit to the Hôtel Dieu they still managed to make. One evening at dinner, after one of these visits, Cécile spoke of an incident that Mother Juschereau had related to her in the morning.

"Father, did you ever hear that once long ago, when an English sailor lay sick at the Hôtel Dieu, Mother Catherine de Saint-Augustin ground up a tiny morsel of bone from Father Brébeuf's skull and mixed it in his gruel, and it made him a Christian?"

Her father looked at her across the table and gave a perplexing chuckle.

"But it is true, certainly? Mother Juschereau told me only today."

"Mother Juschereau and I do not always agree in the

matter of remedies, you know. I consider human bones a very poor medicine for any purpose."

"But he was converted, the sailor. He became a Christian."

"Probably Mother de Saint-Augustin's own saintly character, and her kindness to him, had more to do with the Englishman's conversion than anything she gave him in his food."

"Why, Father, Mother Juschereau would be horrified to hear you! There are so many sacred relics, and they are always working cures."

"The sacred relics are all very well, my dear, and I do not deny that they work miracles,—but not through the digestive tract. Mother de Saint-Augustin meant well, but she made a mistake. If she had given her heretic a little more ground bone, she might have killed him."

"Are you sure?"

"I think it probable. It is true that in England, in every apothecary shop, there is a jar full of pulverized human skulls, and that terrible powder is sometimes dispensed in small doses for certain diseases. Even in France it is still to be found in many pharmacies; but it was never sold in our shop, not even in my grandfather's time. He had seen a proof made of that remedy. A long while ago, when Henry of Navarre was besieging Paris, the people held out against him until they starved by hundreds. I have heard my grandfather tell of things too horrible to repeat to you. The famine grew until there was no food at all;

people killed each other for a morsel. The bakers shut their shops; there was not a handful of flour left, they had used all the forage meant for beasts; they had made bread of hay and straw, and now that was all gone. Then some of the starving went to the cemetery of the Innocents, where there was a great wall of dry bones, and they ground those bones to powder and made a paste of it and baked it in ovens; and as many as ate of that bread died in agony, as if they had swallowed poison. Indeed, they had swallowed poison."

"But those were ordinary bones, maybe bones of wicked people. That would be different."

"No bones are good to be taken into the stomach, Cécile. God did not intend it. The relics of the saints may work cures at the touch, they may be a protection worn about the neck; those things are outside of my knowledge. But I am the guardian of the stomach, and I would not permit a patient to swallow a morsel of any human remains, not those of Saint Peter himself. There are enough beautiful stories about Mother de Saint-Augustin, but this one is not to my liking."

Cécile could only hope it would never happen that her father and Mother Juschereau would enter into any discussion of miraculous cures. Her father must be right; but she felt in her heart that what Mother Juschereau told her had certainly occurred, and the English sailor had been converted by Father Brébeuf's bone.

III

"Ma'm'selle, have you heard the news from Montreal?"

Blinker had just come in for his soup, and Cécile saw that he was greatly excited.

No, she had heard nothing; what did he mean?

"Ma'm'selle, there has been a miracle at Montreal. The recluse has had a visit from the angels,—the night after Epiphany, when there was the big snow-storm. That day she broke her spinning-wheel, and in the night two angels came to her cell and mended it for her. She saw them."

"How did you hear this, Blinker?"

"Some men got in from Montreal this morning, in dog-sledges, and they brought the word. They brought letters, too, for the Reverend Mother at the Ursulines'. If you go there, you will likely hear all about it."

"You are sure she saw the angels?"

He nodded. "Yes, when she got up to pray, at midnight. They say her wheel was mended better than a carpenter could do it."

"The men didn't say which angels, Blinker?"

He shook his head. He was just beginning his soup. Cécile dropped into one of the chairs by the table. "Why, one of them might have been Saint Joseph himself; he was a carpenter. But how was it she saw them? You know she keeps her spinning-wheel up in her work-room, over the cell where she sleeps."

"Just so, ma'm'selle, it is just so the men said. She goes

into the church to pray every night at midnight, and when she got up on Epiphany night, she saw a light shining from the room overhead, and she went up her little stair to see what was the matter, and there she found the angels."

"Did they speak to her?"

"The men did not say. Maybe the Reverend Mother will know."

"I will go there tomorrow, and I will tell you everything I hear. It's a wonderful thing to happen, so near us—and in that great snow-storm! Don't you like to know that the angels are just as near to us here as they are in France?"

Blinker turned his head, glancing all about the kitchen as if someone might be hiding there, leaned across the table, and said to her in such a mournful way:

"Ma'm'selle, I think they are nearer."

When he had drunk his little glass and gone away for the last time, Cécile went in and told her father the good news from Montreal. He listened with polite interest, but she had of late begun to feel that his appreciation of miracles was not at all what it should be. They were reading Plutarch this winter, and tonight they were in the middle of the life of Alexander the Great, but her thoughts strayed from the text. She made so many mistakes that her father said she must be tired, and, gently taking the book from her, continued the reading himself.

Later, while she was undressing, her father filled the

kitchen stove with birch logs to hold the heat well through the night. He blew out the candles, and himself got ready for bed. After he had put on his night-cap and disappeared behind his curtains, Cécile, who had feigned to be asleep, turned over softly to watch the dying fire, and with a sigh abandoned herself to her thoughts. In her mind she went over the whole story of the recluse of Montreal.

Jeanne Le Ber, the recluse, was the only daughter of Jacques Le Ber, the richest merchant of Montreal. When she was twelve years old, her parents had brought her to Quebec and placed her in the Ursuline convent to receive her éducation. She remained here three years, and that was how she belonged to Quebec as well as to Ville-Marie de Montréal. Sister Anne de Sainte-Rose saw at once that this pupil had a very unusual nature, though her outward demeanour was merely that of a charming young girl. The Sister had told Cécile that in those days Jeanne was never melancholy, but warm and ardent, like her complexion; gracious in her manner, and not at all shy. She was at her ease with strangers,—all distinguished visitors to Montreal were entertained at her father's house. But underneath this exterior of pleasing girlhood, Sister Anne felt something reserved and guarded. While she was at the convent, Jeanne often received gifts and attentions from her father's friends in Quebec; and from home, boxes of sweets and dainties. But everything that was sent her she gave away to her schoolmates, so tactfully that they did not realize she kept nothing for herself.

Jeanne completed her studies at the convent, returned home to Montreal, and was in a manner formally introduced to the world there. Her father was fond of society and lavish in hospitality; proud of his five sons, but especially devoted to his only daughter. He loved to see her in rich apparel, and selected the finest stuffs brought over from France for her. Jeanne wore these clothes to please him, but whenever she put on one of her gay dresses, she wore underneath it a little haircloth shirt next her tender skin.

Soon after Jeanne's return from school her father and uncle gave to the newly-completed parish church of Montreal a rich lamp of silver, made in France, to burn perpetually before the Blessed Sacrament. The Le Bers' house on Saint Paul street was very near the church, and from the window of her upstairs bedroom Jeanne could see at night the red spark of the sanctuary lamp showing in the dark church. When everyone was asleep and the house was still, it was her custom to kneel beside her casement and pray, the while watching that spot of light. "*I will be that lamp,*" she used to whisper. "*I will be that lamp; that shall be my life.*"

Jacques Le Ber announced that his daughter's dowry would be fifty thousand gold écus, and there were many pretendants for her hand. Cécile had often heard it said that the most ardent and most favoured of these was Auclair's friend Pierre Charron, who still lived next door to the Le Bers in Montreal. He had been Jeanne's playfellow in childhood.

Jeanne's shining in the *beau monde* of Ville-Marie de Montréal was brief. For her the only real world lay within convent walls. She begged to be allowed to take the vows, but her father's despair overcame her wish. Even her spiritual directors, and that noble soldier-priest Dollier de Casson, Superior of the Sulpician Seminary, advised her against taking a step so irrevocable. She at last obtained her parents' consent to imitate the domestic retreat of Sainte Catherine of Siena, and at seventeen took the vow of chastity for five years and immured herself within her own chamber in her father's house. In her vigils she could always look out at the dark church, with the one constant lamp which generous Jacques Le Ber had placed there, little guessing how it might affect his life and wound his heart.

Upon her retirement Jeanne had explained to her family that during the five years of her vow she must on no account speak to or hold communication with them. Her desire was for the absolute solitariness of the hermit's life, the solitude which Sainte Marie l'Égyptienne had gone into the desert of the Thebais to find. Her parents did not believe that a young girl, affectionate and gentle from her infancy, could keep so harsh a rule. But as time went on, their hearts grew heavier. From the day she took her vow, they never had speech with her or saw her face,— never saw her bodily form, except veiled and stealing down the stairway like a shadow on her way to mass. Jacques Le Ber no longer gave suppers on feast-days. He stayed more and more in his counting-room, drove about in his sledge in winter, and cruised in his sloop in summer; avoided the house that had become the tomb of his hopes.

Before her withdrawal Jeanne had chosen an old serving-woman, exceptional for piety, to give her henceforth such service as was necessary. Every morning at a quarter to five this old dame went to Jeanne's door and attended her to church to hear early mass. Many a time Madame Le Ber concealed herself in the dark hallway to see her daughter's muffled figure go by. After the return from mass, the same servant brought Jeanne her food for the day. If any dish of a rich or delicate nature was brought her, she did not eat it, but fasted.

She went always to vespers, and to the high mass on Sundays and feast-days. On such occasions people used to come in from the neighbouring parishes for a glimpse of that slender figure, the richest heiress in Canada, clad in grey serge, kneeling on the floor near the altar, while her family, in furs and velvet, sat in chairs in another part of the church.

At the end of five years Jeanne renewed her vow of seclusion for another five years. During this time her mother died. On her death-bed she sent one of the household to her daughter's door, begging her to come and give her the kiss of farewell.

"Tell her I am praying for her, night and day," was the answer.

When she had been immured within her father's house for almost ten years, Jeanne was able to accomplish a cherished hope; she devoted that *dot*, which no mortal man would ever claim, to build a chapel for the Sisters of the Congregation of the Blessed Virgin. Behind the high altar of this chapel she had a cell constructed for herself. At a solemn ceremony she took the final vows and entered that cell from which she would never come forth alive. Since that time she had been known as la recluse de Ville-Marie.

Jeanne's entombment and her cell were the talk of the province, and in the country parishes where not much happened, still, after two years, furnished matter for conversation and wonder. The cell, indeed, was not one room, but three, one above another, and within them the solitaire carried on an unvarying routine of life. In the basement cubicle was the grille through which she spoke to her confessor, and by means of which she was actually present at mass and vespers, though unseen. There, through a little window, her meagre food was handed to her. The room above was her sleeping-chamber, constructed by the most careful measurements for one purpose; her narrow bed against the wall was directly behind the high altar, and her pillow, when she slept, was only a few inches from the Blessed Sacrament on the other side of the partition.

The upper cell was her atelier, and there she made and embroidered those beautiful altar-cloths and vestments which went out from her stone chamber to churches all over the province: to the Cathedral at Quebec, and to the poor country parishes where the altar and its ministrant were alike needy. She had begun this work years before, in her father's house, and had grown very skilful at it. Old Bishop Laval, so sumptuous in adorning his Cathedral, had more than once expressed admiration for her beautiful handiwork. When her eyes were tired, or when the day was too dark for embroidering, she spun yarn and knitted stockings for the poor.

In her work-room there was a small iron stove with a heap of faggots, and in the most severe cold of winter the recluse lit a little fire, not for bodily comfort, but because her fingers became stiff with the cold and lost their cunning,—indeed, there were sometimes days on which they would actually have frozen at their task. Every night at midnight, winter and summer, Jeanne rose from her cot, dressed herself, descended into her basement room, opened the grille, and went into the church to pray for an hour before the high altar. On bitter nights many a kind soul in Montreal (and on the lonely farms, too) lay awake for a little, listening to the roar of the storm, and wondered how it was with the recluse, under her single coverlid.

She bore the summer's heat as patiently as the winter's cold. Only last July, when the heat lay so heavy in her chamber with its one small window, her confessor urged her to quit her cell for an hour each day after sunset and take the air in the cloister garden, which her window looked out upon.

She replied: *Ah, mon père, ma chambre est mon paradis terrestre; c'est mon centre; c'est mon élément. Il n'y a pas de lieu plus délicieux, ni plus salutaire pour moi; point de Louvre, point de palais, qui me soit plus agréable. Je préfère ma cellule à tout le reste de l'univers.*

For long after the night when Cécile first heard of the angels' visit to Mademoiselle Le Ber, the story was a joy to her. She told it over and over to little Jacques on his rare visits. Throughout February the weather was so bad that Jacques could come only when Blinker (who was always a match for 'Toinette) went down and brought him up Mountain Hill on his back. The snows fell one upon another until the houses were muffled, the streets like tunnels. Between the storms the weather was grey, with armies of dark clouds moving across the wide sky, and the bitter wind always blowing. Quebec seemed shrunk to a mere group of shivering spires; the whole rock looked like one great white church, above the frozen river.

By many a fireside the story of Jeanne Le Ber's spinning-wheel was told and re-told with loving exaggeration during that severe winter. The word of her visit from the angels went abroad over snow-burdened Canada to the remote parishes. Wherever it went, it brought pleasure, as if the recluse herself had sent to all those families whom she did not know some living beauty,—a blooming rose-tree, or a shapely fruit-tree in fruit. Indeed, she sent them an incomparable gift. In the long evenings, when the family had told over their tales of Indian massacres and lost hunters and the almost human intelligence of the beaver, someone would speak the name of Jeanne Le Ber, and it again gave out fragrance.

The people have loved miracles for so many hundred years, not as proof or evidence, but because they are the actual flowering of desire. In them the vague worship and devotion of the simple-hearted assumes a form. From being a shapeless longing, it becomes a beautiful image; a dumb rapture becomes a melody that can be remembered and repeated; and the experience of a moment, which might have been a lost ecstasy, is made an actual possession and can be bequeathed to another.

IV

One night in March there was a knock at the apothecary's door, just as he was finishing his dinner. Only sick people, or strangers who were ignorant of his habits, disturbed him at that hour. Peeping out between the cabinets, Cécile saw that the visitor was a thick-set man in moccasins, with a bearskin coat and cap. His long hair and his face covered with beard told that he had come in from the woods.

"Don't you remember me, Monsieur Auclair?" he

asked in a low, sad voice. "I am Antoine Frichette; you used to know me."

"It is your beard that changes you, Antoine. Sit down."

"Ah, it is more than that," the man sighed.

"Besides, I thought you were in the Montreal country, —out from the Sault Saint-Louis, wasn't it?"

"Yes, monsieur, I went out there, but I had no luck. My brother-in-law died in the woods, and I got a strain that made me no good, so I came back to live with my sister until I am cured."

"Your brother-in-law? Not Michel Proulx, surely? I am grieved to hear that, Antoine. He cannot well be spared here. We have few such good workmen."

"But you see, monsieur, no building goes on in Kebec in the winter, and there was the chance to make something in the woods. But he is dead, and I am not much better. I got down from Montreal only today,—we had a hard fight coming in this snow. I came to you because I am a sick man. I tore something loose inside me. Look, monsieur, can you do anything for that?" He stood up and unbuttoned his bearskin jacket. A rupture, Auclair saw at once,—and for a woodsman that was almost like a death-sentence.

Yes, he told Frichette, he could certainly do something for him. But first they would be seated more comfortably, and have a talk. He took the poor fellow back into the sitting-room and gave him his own arm-chair by the fire.

"This is my daughter, Cécile, Antoine; you remember

her. Now I will give you something to make you feel better at once. This is a very powerful cordial, there are many healing herbs in it, and it will reach the sorest spot in a sick man. Drink it slowly, and then you must tell me about your bad winter."

The woodsman took the little glass between his thick fingers and held it up to the fire-light. "*C'est jolie, la couleur,*" he observed childishly. Presently he slid off his fur jacket and sat in his buckskin shirt and breeches. When he had finished the cordial, his host filled his glass again, and Antoine sighed and looked about him. "*C'est tranquille, chez vous, comme toujours,*" he said with a faint smile. "I bring you a message, monsieur, from Father Hector Saint-Cyr."

"From Father Hector? You have seen him? Come, Cécile, Antoine is going to tell us news of our friend." Auclair rose and poured a little cordial for himself.

"He said he will be here very soon, God willing, while the river is still hard. He had a letter from the new Bishop telling him to come down to Kebec. He asked me to say that he invited himself to dinner with you. He is a man in a thousand, that priest. We have been through something together. But that is a long story."

"Begin at the beginning, Frichette, my daughter and I have all evening to listen. So you and Proulx went into the woods, out from the Sault?"

"Yes, we went early in the fall, when the hunting was good, and we took Joseph Choret from Three Rivers.

We put by plenty of fish, as soon as it was cold enough to freeze them. We meant to go up into the Nipissing country in the spring, and trade for skins. The Nipissings don't come to the settlements much, and I know a little of their language. We made a good log house in the fall, good enough, but you know what a man my brother-in-law was for hewing; he wasn't satisfied. When the weather kept open, before Christmas, he wanted to put in a board floor. I cannot say how it happened. You know yourself, monsieur, what a man he was with the ax,—he hewed the beams for Notre Dame de la Victoire when he was but a lad, and how many houses in Kebec didn't he hew the beams and flooring for? He could cut better boards with his ax than most men can with a saw. He was not a drinking man, either; never took a glass too much. Very well; one day out there he was hewing boards to floor our shack, and something happens,—the ax slips and lays his leg open from the ankle to the knee. There is a big vein spouting blood, and I catch it and tie it with a deer-gut string I had in my pocket. Maybe that gut was poisoned some way, for the wound went bad very soon. We had no linen, so I dressed it with punk wood, as the Indians do. I boiled pine chips and made turpentine, but it did no good. He got black to the thigh and began to suffer agony. The only thing that eased him was fresh snow heaped on his leg. I don't know if it was right, but he begged for it. After Christmas I saw it was time to get a priest.

"It was three days' journey in to the Sault mission, and the going was bad. There wasn't snow enough for snow-shoes,—just enough to cover the roots and trip you. I took my snowshoes and grub-sack on my back, and made good time. The second day I came to a place where the trees were thin because there was no soil, only flint rock, in ledges. And there one big tree, a white pine, had blown over. It hadn't room to fall flat, the top had caught in the branches of another tree, so it lay slanting and made a nice shelter underneath, like a shanty, high enough to stand in. The top was still fresh and green and made thick walls to keep out the wind. I cleared away some of the inside branches and had a good sleep in there. Next morning when I left that place, I notched a few trees as I went, so I could find it when I brought the priest back with me. Ordinarily I don't notch trees to find my way back. When there is no sun, I can tell directions like the Indians."

Here Auclair interrupted him. "And how is that, Antoine?"

Frichette smiled and shrugged. "It is hard to explain,—by many things. The limbs of the trees are generally bigger on the south side, for example. The moss on the trunks is clean and dry on the north side,—on the south side it is softer and maybe a little rotten. There are many little signs; put them all together and they point you right.

"I got to the mission late the third night and slept in a bed. Early the next morning Father Hector was ready to start back with me. He had two young priests there, but he would go himself. He carried his snowshoes and a blanket and the Blessed Sacrament on his back, and I carried the provisions—smoked eels and cold grease—enough for three days. We slept the first night in that shelter under the fallen pine, and made a good start the next day. That was Epiphany, the day of the big snow all over Canada. When we had been out maybe two hours, the snow began to fall so thick we could hardly see each other, and I told Father Hector we better make for that shelter again. It took us nearly all day to get back over the ground we had covered in two hours before the storm began. By God, I was glad to see that thin place in the woods again! I was afraid I'd lost it. There was our tree, heaped over with snow, with the opening to the south still clear. We crept in and got our breath and unrolled our blankets. A little snow had sifted in, but not much. It had packed between the needles of that pine top until it was like a solid wall and roof. It was warm in there; no wind got through. Father Hector said some prayers, and we rolled up in our blankets and slept most of the day and let the storm come.

"Next day it was still snowing hard, and I was afraid to start out. We ate some lard, and an eel apiece, but I could see the end of our provisions pretty soon. We were thirsty and ate the snow, which doesn't satisfy you much. Father Hector said prayers and read his breviary. When I went to sleep, I heard him praying to himself, very low,—and when I wakened he was still praying, just the same. I lay still and listened for a long while, but I didn't once hear an Ave Maria, and not the name of a saint could I make out. At last I turned over and told Father Hector that was certainly a long prayer he was saying. He laughed. 'That's not a prayer, Antoine,' he says; 'that's a Latin poem, a very long one, that I learned at school. If I am uncomfortable, it diverts my mind, and I remember my old school and my comrades.'

" 'So much the better for you, Father,' I told him. 'But a long prayer would do no harm. I don't like the look of things.'

"The next day the snow had stopped, but a terrible bitter wind was blowing. We couldn't have gone against it, but since it was behind us, I thought we'd better get ahead. We hadn't food enough to see us through, as it was. That was a cruel day's march on an empty belly. Father Hector is a good man on snowshoes, and brave, too. My pack had grown lighter, and I wanted to carry his, but he would not have it. When it began to get dark, we made camp and ate some cold grease and the last of our eels. I built a fire, and we took turns, one of us feeding the fire while the other slept. I was so tired I could have slept on into eternity. Father Hector had to throw snow in my face to waken me.

"Before daylight the wind died, but the cold was so bitter we had to move or freeze. It was good snowshoe-ing that day, but with empty bellies and thirst and eating snow, we both had colic. That night we ate the last of our lard. I wasn't sure we were going right,—the snow had changed the look of everything. When Father Hector took off the little box he carried that held the Blessed Sacrament, I said: 'Maybe that will do for us two, Father. I don't see much ahead of us.'

" 'Never fear, Antoine,' says he, 'while we carry that, Someone is watching over us. Tomorrow will bring better luck.'

"It did, too, just as he said. We were both so weak we made poor headway. But by the mercy of God we met an Indian. He had a gun, and he had shot two hares. When he saw what a bad way we were in, he made a fire very quick and cooked the hares,—and he ate very little of that meat himself. He said Indians could bear hunger better than the French. He was a kind Indian and was glad to give us what he had. Father Hector could speak his language, and questioned him. Though I had never seen him before, he knew where our shack was, and said we were pointed right. But I told him I was tired out and wanted a guide, and I would pay him well in shot and powder if he took us in.

"We got back to our shack six days after we left the mission, and they were the six worst days of the winter. My brother-in-law was very bad. He died while Father Hector was there, and had a Christian burial. The Indian took Father Hector back to the mission. Soon after that I got this strain in my side, and I lost heart. I left our stores for Joseph Choret to trade with, and I went down to the Sault and then to Montreal. I found a sledge party about to come down the river, and they brought me to Kebec. Now I am here, what can you do for me, Monsieur Auclair?"

The apothecary's kindly tone did not reassure Frichette. He looked searchingly into his face and asked:

"Will it grow back, my inside, like it was?"

Auclair felt very sorry for him. "No, it will not grow back, Antoine. But tomorrow I will make you a support, and you will be more comfortable."

"But not to carry canoes over portages, I guess? No? Nor to go into the woods at all, maybe?" He sank back in the chair. "Then I don't know how I'll make a living, monsieur. I am not clever with tools, like my brother-in-law."

"We'll find a way out of that, Antoine."

Frichette did not heed him. "It's a funny thing," he went on. "A man sits here by the warm fire, where he can hear the bell ring for mass every morning and smell bread baked fresh every day, and all that happened out there in the woods seems like a dream. Yet here I am, no good any more."

"*Courage, mon bourgeois*, I am going to give you a good medicine."

Frichette shook his head and spread his thick fingers apart on his knees. "There is no future for me if I cannot paddle a canoe up the big rivers any more."

"Perhaps you can paddle, Antoine, but not carry."

Antoine rose. "In this world, who paddles must carry, monsieur. Good night, Mademoiselle Cécile. Father Hector will be surprised to see how you have grown. He thinks a great deal about that good dinner you are going to give him, I expect. You ask him if it tastes as good as those hares the Indian cooked for him when he was out with Frichette."

V

Father Hector Saint-Cyr was not long in following his messenger. On the day of his arrival in Kebec he stopped at the apothecary shop, but, Auclair being out, he saw only Cécile, and they arranged that he should come to dinner the following evening.

He came after hearing vespers at the Cathedral, attended to the door of the pharmacy by a group of Seminarians, who always followed him about when he was in town. This was his first meeting with Auclair, and there was a cordial moisture in the priest's eyes as he embraced his old friend and kissed him on both cheeks.

"How many times on my way from Ville-Marie I have enjoyed this moment in anticipation, Euclide," he declared. "Only solitary men know the full joys of friendship. Others have their family; but to a solitary and an exile his friends are everything."

Father Hector was the son of a noted family of Aix-en-Provence; his good breeding and fine presence were by no means lost upon his Indian parishioners at the Sault. The savages, always scornful of meekness and timidity, believed that a man was exactly what he looked. They used Father Hector better than any of his predecessors because he was strong and fearless and handsome. If he was humble before Heaven, he was never so with his converts. He took a high hand with them. If one were drunk or impertinent, he knocked him down. More than once he had given a drunken Indian a good beating, and the Indian had come and thanked him afterwards, telling him he did quite right.

Cécile thought it a great honour to entertain a man like Father Hector at their table, and she was much gratified by his frank enjoyment of everything; of the fish soup with which she had taken such pains, and the wood doves, cooked in a casserole with mushrooms and served with wild rice. Her father had brought up from the cellar a bottle of fine old Burgundy which the Count had sent them for New Year's. She scarcely ate at all herself, for watching their guest.

When Auclair said that this dinner was to make up to Father Hector for the one he missed on Epiphany, he laughed and protested that on Epiphany he had dined very well.

"Smoked eels and cold lard—what more does a man want in the woods? It was on the day following that we began to feel the pinch,—and the next day, and the next. Frichette made a great fuss about it, but certainly it was

not the first time either he or I had gone hungry. If one
had not been through little experiences of that kind, one
would not know how to enjoy a dinner like this." He
reached out and put his hand lightly on Cécile's head.
"How I wish you could keep her from growing up,
Euclide!"

She blushed with joy at the touch of that large, handsome hand which the Indians feared.

"Yes," he went on, looking about him, "these are great
occasions in a missionary's life. The next time I am over-
taken by a storm in the woods, the recollection of this
evening will be food and warmth to me. I shall see it in
memory as plainly as I see it now; this room, so like at
home, this table with everything as it should be; and,
most of all, the feeling of being with one's own kind.
How many times, out there, I shall live over this evening
again, with you and Cécile." Father Hector tasted his
wine, inhaling it with a deep breath. "Very clearly, Euclide, it was arranged in Heaven that I should be a missionary in a foreign land. I am peculiarly susceptible to
the comforts of the fireside and to the charm of children.
If I were a teacher in the college at home, where I have
many young nieces and nephews, I should be always
planning for them. I should sink into nepotism, the most
disastrous of the failings of the popes."

Auclair had to remind Cécile when it was time to bring
in the dessert. She had quite forgot where they were in
the dinner, so intent was she upon Father Hector's talk,

upon watching his brown face and white forehead, with a sweep of black hair standing out above it.

"And now, Cécile," said her father, "shall we tell Father Hector our secret? Next autumn the Count expects to return to France, and we go with him. We think you have been a missionary long enough; that it is time for you to become a professor of rhetoric again. We expect you to go back with us,—or very soon afterwards."

Father Hector smiled, but shook his head. "Ah, no. Thank you, but no. I have taken a vow that will spoil your plans for me. I shall not return to France."

Auclair had put his glass to his lips, but set it down untasted. "Not return?" he echoed.

"Not at all, Euclide; never."

"But when my wife was here, you both used to plan—"

"Ah, yes. That was my temptation. Now it is vanquished." He sat for a moment smiling. Then he began resolutely:

"Listen, my friend. No man can give himself heart and soul to one thing while in the back of his mind he cherishes a desire, a secret hope, for something very different. You, as a student, must know that even in worldly affairs nothing worth while is accomplished except by that last sacrifice, the giving of oneself altogether and finally. Since I made that final sacrifice, I have been twice the man I was before."

Auclair felt disturbed, a little frightened. "You have made a vow, you say? Is it irrevocable?"

"Irrevocable. And what do you suppose gave me the strength to make that decision? Why, merely a good example!" At this point Father Hector glanced at Cécile and saw that she had almost ceased to breathe in her excitement; that her eyes, in the candlelight, were no longer blue, but black. Again he put out his hand and touched her head. "See, she understands me! From the beginning women understand devotion, it is a natural grace with them; they have only to learn where to direct it. Men have to learn everything.

"There was among the early missionaries, among the martyrs, one whom I have selected for my especial reverence. I mean Noël Chabanel, Euclide. He was not so great a figure as Brébeuf or Jogues or Lalemant, but I feel a peculiar sympathy for him. He perished, you remember, in the great Iroquois raid of '49. But his martyrdom was his life, not his death.

"He was a little different from all the others,—equal to them in desire, but not in fitness. He was only thirty years of age when he came, and was from Toulouse, that gracious city.

"Chabanel had been a professor of rhetoric like me, and like me he was fond of the decencies, the elegancies of life. From the beginning his life in Canada was one long humiliation and disappointment. Strange to say, he was utterly unable to learn the Huron language, though he was a master of Greek and Hebrew and spoke both Italian and Spanish. After five years of devoted study he was still unable to converse or to preach in any Indian tongue. He was sent out to the mission of Saint Jean in the Tobacco nation, as helper to Father Charles Garnier. Father Garnier, though not at all Chabanel's equal in scholarship, had learned the Huron language so thoroughly that the Indians said there was nothing more to teach him,—he spoke like one of themselves.

"His humiliating inability to learn the language was only one of poor Chabanel's mortifications. He had no love for his converts. Everything about the savages and their mode of life was utterly repulsive and horrible to him; their filth, their indecency, their cruelty. The very smell of their bodies revolted him to nausea. He could never feel toward them that long-suffering love which has been the consolation of our missionaries. He never became hardened to any of the privations of his life, not even to the vermin and mosquitos that preyed upon his body, nor to the smoke and smells in the savage wigwams. In his struggle to learn the language he went and lived with the Indians, sleeping in their bark shelters, crowded with dogs and dirty savages. Often Father Chabanel would lie out in the snow until he was in danger of a death self-inflicted, and only then creep inside the wigwam. The food was so hateful to him that one might say he lived upon fasting. The flesh of dogs he could never eat without becoming ill, and even corn-meal boiled in dirty water and dirty kettles brought on vomiting; so that he used to beg the women to give him a little uncooked meal in his hand, and upon that he subsisted.

"The Huron converts were more brutal to him than to Father Garnier. They were contemptuous of his backwardness in their language, and they must have divined his excessive sensibility, for they took every occasion to outrage it. In the wigwam they tirelessly perpetrated indecencies to wound him. Once when a hunting party returned after a long famine, they invited him to a feast of flesh. After he had swallowed the portion in his bowl, they pulled a human hand out of the kettle to show him that he had eaten of an Iroquois prisoner. He became ill at once, and they followed him into the forest to make merry over his retchings.

"But through all these physical sufferings, which remained as sharp as on the first day, the greatest of his sufferings was an almost continual sense of the withdrawal of God. All missionaries have that anguish at times, but with Chabanel it was continual. For long months, for a whole winter, he would exist in the forest, every human sense outraged, and with no assurance of the nearness of God. In those seasons of despair he was constantly beset by temptation in the form of homesickness. He longed to leave the mission to priests who were better suited to its hardships, to return to France and teach the young, and to find again that peace of soul, that cleanliness and order, which made him the master of his mind and its powers. Everything that he had lost was awaiting him in France, and the Director of Missions in Quebec had suggested his return.

"On Corpus Christi Day, in the fifth year of his labours in Canada and the thirty-fifth of his age, he cut short this struggle and overcame his temptation. At the mission of Saint Matthias, in the presence of the Blessed Sacrament exposed, he made a vow of perpetual stability (*perpetuam stabilitatem*) in the Huron missions. This vow he recorded in writing, and he sent copies of it to his brethren in Kebec.

"Having made up his mind to die in the wilderness, he had not long to wait. Two years later he perished when the mission of Saint Jean was destroyed by the Iroquois,— though whether he died of cold in his flight through the forest, or was murdered by a faithless convert for the sake of the poor belongings he carried on his back, was not surely known. No man ever gave up more for Christ than Noël Chabanel; many gave all, but few had so much to give.

"It was perhaps in memory of his sufferings that I, in my turn, made a vow of perpetual stability. For those of us who are unsteadfast by nature, who have other lawful loves than our devotion to our converts, it is perhaps the safest way. My sacrifice is poor compared with his. I was able to learn the Indian languages; I have a house where I can, at least, pray in solitude; I can keep clean, and am seldom hungry except by accident in the journeys I have to make. But Noël Chabanel—ah, when your faith is cold, think of him! How can there be men in France this day who doubt the existence of God, when for the love of Him weak human beings have been able to endure so much?"

Cécile looked up at him in bewilderment. "Are there such men, Father?" she whispered.

"There are, my child,—but it is the better for you if you have never heard of them."

Presently it was time that Father Hector should get back to Monseigneur de Saint-Vallier's Palace, where he was lodged during his stay in Quebec.

"And your books, Father Hector? Will you not take them back to the Sault with you? If I leave Canada before you visit Quebec again, what shall I do with them?" Auclair opened a cabinet and pointed to a row of volumes bound in vellum. Father Hector's eyes brightened as he looked at them, but he shook his head.

"No, I shall not take them this time. If you go away, give them to Monseigneur l'Ancien to keep for me. If they could be eaten, or worn on the back, he would give them to the poor, certainly. But Greek and Latin texts will be safe with him. I will not say good-bye, for I shall come tomorrow to lay in a supply of medicines for my mission."

After Auclair had disappeared behind his bed-curtains that night, he lay awake a long while, regretting that a man with Father Hector's gifts should decide to live and die in the wilderness, and wondering whether there had not been a good deal of misplaced heroism in the Canadian missions,—a waste of rare qualities which did nobody any good.

"Ah, well," he sighed at last, "perhaps that is the box of precious ointment which was acceptable to the Saviour, and I am like the disciples who thought it might have been used better in another way."

This solution allowed him to go to sleep.

VI

About the middle of March, soon after Father Hector's visit, the weather went sick, as it were. The air suddenly grew warm and springlike, and for three days there was a continuous downpour of rain. The deep snow drank it up like a thirsty sponge, but never melted. Not a patch of ground showed through, even on the hill-sides. But the snow darkened; everything grew grey like faintly smoked glass. The ice in the river broke up before Quebec, and olive-green water carried grey islands of ice and snow slowly northward. The great pine forests, across the river and on the western sky-line, were no longer bronze, but black. The only colours in the world were black and white and grey,—bewildering variations of clouded white and grey. The Laurentian mountains, to the north, sometimes showed a little blue in their valleys, when the fogs thinned enough to let them be seen. After the interval of rain everything froze hard again and stayed frozen,—but no fresh snow fell. The white winter was gone. Only the smirched ruins of winter remained, mournful and bleak and impoverished, frozen into enduring solidity.

Behind the Auclairs' little back yard and the baker's, the cliff ran up to the Château in a perpendicular wall, and the face of it was overgrown with wild cherry bushes and knotty little Canadian willows. It was up there that one looked, from the back door, for the first sign of spring. But all through April those stumps and twigs were so forbidding, so black and ugly, that Cécile often wondered whether anything short of a miracle of the old-fashioned kind could ever make the sap rise in them again.

A great many people in the town were sick at this time, and Cécile herself caught a cold and was feverish. Her father wrapped her in blankets and made her sit with her feet in a hot mustard bath while she drank a great quantity of sassafras tea. Then he put her to bed and entertained her with an account of the cures his father and grandfather had effected with sassafras. It was one of the medicinal plants of the New World in which he had great faith. It had been first brought to Europe by Sir Walter Raleigh, he said, and had been for a time a very popular remedy in France. Even when it went out of fashion, the pharmacy on the Quai des Célestins had remained loyal to it, and continued to use sassafras after it became expensive because of infrequent supply. His father got it from London, where it still came in occasional shipments from the Virginia colony.

Cécile was kept in bed for three days,—in her father's big bed, with the curtains drawn back, while her father himself attended to all the household duties. He was an accomplished cook, and continual practice in making medicines kept his hand expert in handling glass and earthenware and in regulating heat. He debated the advisability of sending for Jeanette, the laundress, or of asking Madame Pigeon to come in and help him. "*Mais non, nous sommes plus tranquilles comme ça,*" he decided. That was the important thing—tranquillity. In the evenings he read aloud to his daughter; and even when he was in the shop, she could hear everything his clients had to say, so she was not dull. If her father was disengaged for a moment, he came in to chat with her. They talked about Father Hector, and of how soon they could hope for green salads in the market, and of whether it could be true that Pierre Charron was home from the Great Lakes already, since there was a rumour that he had been seen in Montreal.

It was a pleasant and a novel experience to lie warm in bed while her father was getting dinner in the kitchen, and to feel no responsibility at all; to listen to the drip of the rain, to watch the grey daylight fade away in the salon, and the firelight grow redder and redder on the old chairs and the sofa, on the gilt picture-frames and the brass candlesticks. But her mind roamed about the town and was dreamily conscious of its activities and of the lives of her friends; of the dripping grey roofs and spires, the lighted windows along the crooked streets, the great grey river choked with ice and frozen snow, the never-ending, merciless forest beyond. All these things seemed to her like layers and layers of shelter, with this one flickering, shadowy room at the core.

They dined on the little table beside the bed (as they so often breakfasted even when she was well), and after dinner her father closed the door so that she would not be disturbed by the noise he made in washing the dishes, or even by Blinker's visit. It was while he was thus alone in the kitchen that he had, one evening, a strange interview with Blinker.

When Blinker had finished his tasks, he asked timidly if monsieur would please give him a little of that medicine again, to make him sleep.

Auclair looked at him doubtfully.

"How long is it you have not been sleeping?"

"Oh, a long time! Please, monsieur, give me something."

"Sit down, Jules. What is the matter? You are strong and healthy. You do not overeat. I cannot understand why you have this trouble. Perhaps you have something on your mind."

"Perhaps."

"That will often keep one awake. I am not a man to meddle, but if you told me what worries you, I should know better what to do for you."

Blinker's head drooped. He looked very miserable.

"Monsieur, I am an unfortunate man. If I told you, you might put me out."

"You have told your confessor?"

"It was not a sin. Not what they call a sin. It was a misfortune."

"Well, we will never put you out, Jules, be sure of that."

Blinker, with his hands knotted on his knees, seemed to be trying to bring something up out of himself. "Monsieur," he said at last, "I am unfortunate. I was brought up to a horrible trade. I was a torturer in the King's prison at Rouen."

Auclair started, but he caught himself quickly.

"Well, Jules," he said quietly, "that, too, is the King's service."

"*Sale service, monsieur,*" the poor wretch exclaimed bitterly, "*sale métier!* It was my father who did those things,—he was under the chief, he had to do it. I was afraid of him, for he was a hard man. I had no chance to learn another trade. Nobody wanted the prison folks about. In the street people would curse us. My father gave me brandy when he made me help him, all I could hold. He said it was right to punish the wicked, but I could never get used to it. Then something dreadful happened." Blinker was shivering all over.

Auclair poured him a glass of spirits and put some more wood into the stove. "You had better get it out, my boy. That will help you," he told him.

Hard as it was for Blinker to talk, he managed to tell his story. In Rouen there was a rough sort of woman who lived down near the river and did washing. She was honest, but quarrelsome; her neighbours didn't like her. She had a little son who was a bad boy, and she often thrashed him. When he grew older, he struck back, and they used to fight, to the great annoyance of the neighbours. One summer this boy disappeared. A search was made for him. His mother was examined, and contradicted herself. The neighbours remembered hearing angry shouts and a smashing of bottles one night; they began to say she had done away with him. Someone made an accusation. The laundress was taken before the examiners again, but was sullen and refused to talk. She was put to the torture. After half an hour she broke down and confessed that she had killed her son, had put his body into a sack with stones and dragged it to the river. A few weeks later she was hanged.

Not long afterwards Blinker began to have trouble with his lower jaw, some decomposition of the bone; pieces of bone came out through his cheek. For weeks he never lay down, but walked the floor all night. Sometimes when he was full of brandy, he could doze in a chair for half an hour.

But he had another misery, harder to bear than his jaw. This was the first time he had ever suffered great pain, and ghosts began to haunt him. The faces of people he had put to torture rose before him, faces he had long forgotten. When everybody else was asleep, he could think of nothing but those faces. He told himself it was the law of the land and must be right; someone had to do it. But they never gave him any peace.

The suppuration in his jaw stopped at last. The scars on his face had begun to heal, when that murdered boy came back,—walked insolently in the streets of Rouen. The truth came out. After his quarrel with his mother he had hidden himself away on a boat tied up to the wharf, had got to Le Havre undiscovered, and there shipped as *mousse* on a bark bound for the West Indies. He made the voyage and came home.

Blinker began to walk the floor at night again, just as when his jaw was at its worst. How many of the others had been innocent? He could never get the big washer-woman's screams out of his ears. He would have made away with himself then, but he was afraid of being punished after death. If he dropped asleep from exhaustion, he would dream of her. He had only one hope; that miserable boy's adventure had put a thought into his head. If he could get away to a new country, where nobody knew him for the executioner's son, perhaps he would leave all that behind and forget it. That was why he had come to Kebec. But sometimes, he never knew when or why, these things would rise up out of the past . . . faces . . . voices . . . even words, things they had said.

"They are inside me, monsieur, I carry them with me."

Blinker closed his eyes and slowly dropped his head forward on his hands.

"Your sickness was a good chance for you, my poor fellow. Suffering teaches us compassion. There are some in Kebec, in high places, who have not learned that yet. If Monseigneur de Saint-Vallier had ever known chagrin and disappointment, he would not cross the old Bishop as he does. I will give you something to make you sleep tomorrow, but afterwards you will not need anything. When God sent you that affliction in your face, he showed his mercy to you. And, by the way, who is your confessor?"

"Father Sébastien, at the Récollets'. But I have wanted to tell you, monsieur, ever since All Souls' Eve. I came back late with my buckets, and the door there was a little open,—you were telling Ma'm'selle about the old man who stole the brass pots. I wanted to make away with myself—but you said something. You said the law was wrong, not us poor creatures. Monsieur, I never hurt an animal to amuse myself, as some do. I was brought up to that trade." Blinker stopped and wiped the sweat out of his eyes with his sleeve.

The poor fellow had begun to give off a foul odour, as creatures do under fear or anguish. Auclair watched with amazement the twisted face he saw every day above an armful of wood,—grown as familiar to him as an ugly piece of furniture,—now become altogether strange; it brought to his mind terrible weather-worn stone faces on the churches at home,—figures of the tormented in scenes of the Last Judgment. He hastened to measure out a dose of laudanum. After Blinker had gone out of the kitchen door, he made the sign of the cross over his own heart before he blew out the candle and went in to his daughter.

Cécile was flushed and excited; she had been crying, he saw.

"Oh father, why were you so long with Blinker, and what was he telling you? He sounded so miserable!"

Her father put her head back on the pillow and smoothed her hair. "He was telling me all his old troubles, my dear, and when you are well again, I will tell them to you. We must be very kind to him. Your mother was right when she said there was no harm in him. Tomorrow I will go to Father Sébastien, and between us we will cure his distress."

"Then it was not a crime? You know some people say he was in the galleys in France."

"No, he was never in the galleys. He was one of the unfortunate of this world. You remember, when Queen Dido offers Æneas hospitality, she says: *Having known misery, I have learned to pity the miserable.* Our poor wood-carrier is like Queen Dido."

The next morning Cécile's recovery began. As soon as she had drunk her chocolate, her father brought a pair of woollen stockings and told her to put them on. When she looked up at him wonderingly, he said:

"I have something to show you."

He wrapped her in a blanket, took her up in his arms, and carried her into the kitchen, where the back door stood open.

"Look out yonder," he said, "and presently you will see something."

She looked out at the dreary cliff-side with its black, frozen bushes and dirty snow, and long, grey icicles hanging from the jagged rocks. She wondered if there could be yellow buds on the willows, perhaps; but they were still naked, like stiff black briars.

Suddenly there was a movement up there, a flicker of something swift and slender in the grey light, against the grey, granulated snow,—then a twitter, a scolding anxious protest. Now she knew why her father had smiled so confidently when he lifted her out of bed.

"Oh, Papa, it is our swallow! Then the spring is coming! Nothing can keep it back now." She put her head down on his shoulder and cried a little. He pretended not to notice it, but stood holding her fast, patting her back, so muffled in folds of blanket.

"She is hunting her old nest, up among the crags. I cannot see whether it is still there. But if it has been blown away, she can easily build herself another. She can get mud, because there is a thaw every day now about noon, and the dead leaves are sticking up wherever the snow melts."

"Is she the only one? Is she all alone?"

"She is the only one here this morning, but her friends will be close behind. Listen, how she scolds!"

"Father," said Cécile suddenly, "where has she been, our swallow? Where, do you think?"

"Oh, far away in the South! Somewhere down there where Robert de La Salle was murdered. By the Gulf of Mexico, perhaps."

"And in France where do the swallows go in winter?"

"Very far. Across the Mediterranean to Algérie, where the oranges grow."

"Has our swallow been where there are oranges? Do they grow by the Gulf of Mexico? Oh, Papa, I wish I could see an orange, on its little tree!"

"You will see them when we go home. There are fine old orange-trees growing under glass in our own parish, and they are brought out into the courtyards in summer."

"But couldn't we possibly grow one here in Quebec? The Jesuits have such great warm cellars; I am sure they could, if they tried."

Her father laughed as he carried her back to bed. "I am afraid not even the Jesuits could do that! Now I am going to leave you for a little while. I will put a card on the door announcing that we are closed until noon. You are so much better, that I can make my visit to the Hôtel Dieu this morning."

"And on your way, Papa, will you stop and tell Monseigneur l'Ancien that our swallow has come? For his book, you know."

Ever since he first came out to Canada, old Bishop Laval had kept a brief weather record, noting down the date of the first snowfall, when the river froze over, the nights of excessive cold, the storms and the great thaws. And for nearly forty years now he had faithfully recorded the return of the swallow.

BOOK IV
PIERRE CHARRON

BOOK FOUR

PIERRE CHARRON

I

It was the first day of June. Before dawn a wild calling and twittering of birds in the bushes on the cliff-side above the apothecary's back door announced clear weather. When the sun came up over the Île d'Orléans, the rock of Kebec stood gleaming above the river like an altar with many candles, or like a holy city in an old legend, shriven, sinless, washed in gold. The quickening of all life and hope which had come to France in May had reached the far North at last. That morning the Auclairs drank their chocolate with all the doors and windows open.

Euclide was at his desk, making up little packets of saffron flowers to flavour fish soups, when a slender man in buckskins, with a quick swinging step, crossed the threshold and embraced him before he had time to rise. He was not a big fellow, this Pierre Charron, hero of the fur trade and the coureurs de bois, not above medium height, but quick as an otter and always sure of himself. When Auclair, after returning his embrace with delight, drew back to look at him and asked him how he was, he threw up his chin and answered:

"*Je me porte bien, comme toujours.*"

"And have you had a good winter, Pierre?"

"But yes. I always have a good winter, monsieur. I see to it."

"And how do you happen to be down so early?"

Charron's face changed. He frowned. "That is not so good. My mother was ailing. They brought me word, out to Michilimackinac, so I returned to Montreal in March. She was better; the Sisters of the Congregation had been taking care of her. But I did not leave her again. No one can nurse her so well as I. I stayed at home and let the other fellows have my spring trade this year. I can afford it."

"But I must hear about your mother's ailment, my son; and first let me call Cécile. She will not want to lose even a minute of your visit."

Auclair went back to the kitchen, and Cécile ran in without stopping to take off her *tablier*. It flashed across Pierre that she was perhaps growing too tall to be kissed. But she was quicker than his thought, threw her arms about his neck, and gave him the glad kiss of welcome.

"Oh, Pierre Charron, I am delighted at you, Pierre Charron!"

He stood laughing, holding both her hands and swinging them back and forth in a rhythm of some sort, so that though they were standing still, they seemed to be dancing. Cécile was laughing, too, as children do where they never have been afraid or uncertain. "Oh, Pierre, have you been to the great falls again, and Michilimackinac?"

"Everywhere, everywhere!" He swung her hands faster and faster.

"And you will tell me about the big beaver towns?"

"Gently, Cécile," her father interposed. "Pierre's mother has been ill, and he will tell us first about her. What was it like this time, my boy, a return of her old complaint?" The one long journey Auclair had ever made away from Quebec since he landed here was to go up to Montreal in Pierre's shallop to examine and prescribe for Madame Charron.

From his first meeting with him, Auclair had loved this restless boy (he was a boy then) who shot up and down the swift rivers of Canada in his canoe; who was now at Niagara, now at the head of Lake Ontario, now at the Sault Sainte Marie on his way into the fathomless forbidding waters of Lake Superior. To both Auclair and Madame Auclair, Pierre Charron had seemed the type they had come so far to find; more than anyone else he realized the romantic picture of the free Frenchman of the great forests which they had formed at home on the bank of the Seine. He had the good manners of the Old World, the dash and daring of the New. He was proud, he was vain, he was relentless when he hated, and quickly prejudiced; but he had the old ideals of clan-loyalty, and in friendship he never counted the cost. His goods and his life were at the disposal of the man he loved or the leader he admired. Though his figure was still boyish, his face was full of experience and sagacity; a fine bold nose, a restless, rather mischievous mouth, white teeth, very strong and even, sparkling hazel eyes with a kind of living flash in them, like the sunbeams on the bright rapids upon which he was so skilful.

Pierre's father, a soldier of fortune from Languedoc, had done well in the fur trade and built himself a comfortable dwelling in Montreal, on Saint Paul street, next the house of Jacques Le Ber. Pierre was almost exactly the same age as Le Ber's daughter, Jeanne; the two children had been playmates and had learned their catechism together. After Pierre's father was drowned in a storm on Lake Ontario, Jacques Le Ber took the son into his employ to train him for the fur business. Of all the suitors for Mademoiselle Le Ber's hand Pierre was thought to have the best chance of success, and the merchant would have liked him for a son-in-law. At the time when Mademoiselle Le Ber, then fifteen, came home from her schooling in Quebec, Pierre was her father's clerk and was often at the house. She had seemed favourably disposed toward him. It was an old story in Montreal that after Jeanne took her first vow and immured herself in her father's house, disappointment had driven young Charron into the woods. He had learned the Indian languages as a child, and the Indians liked and trusted him, as they had liked his father. All along the Great Lakes, as far as Michilimackinac, he had a name among them for courage and fair dealing, for a loyal friend and a relentless enemy. Every year he gave half the profits of his ventures to his mother; the rest he squandered on drink and women and new guns, as his comrades did. But in Montreal his behaviour was always exemplary, out of respect to his mother.

After accepting Auclair's invitation to come to supper that evening, Charron said he must go to Noël Pommier to order a pair of hard boots,—he was wearing moccasins. "And will you come along, little monkey?" he asked, making a face. When Cécile was little, he had always called her his *petit singe*.

She glanced eagerly at her father. He nodded. "Run along, and give my respects to Madame Pommier."

Cécile slipped her hand into Charron's, and they went out into the street. Across the way, they saw Monseigneur de Saint-Vallier in his garden, directing some workmen who were apparently building an arbour for him.

"I see your grand neighbour has come home," Pierre observed.

"Oh yes, last September. But you must have heard?

People say he brought such beautiful things for his house; furniture and paintings and tapestry and silver dishes. Wouldn't you love to see the inside of his Palace?"

"Not a bit! He is too French for me." Charron threw up his chin.

Cécile laughed. "But my father is French, and so is Father Hector; you like them."

"Oh, that is different. But the man over there goes against me. He smells of Versailles. The old man is my Bishop. But I could do without any of them."

"Hush, Pierre Charron! You are foolish to quarrel with the priests. I love Father Hector. You can't say he isn't a brave man."

Pierre shrugged. "Oh, he is brave enough. All the same, he's a little too Frenchified for me. You and I are Canadians, monkey. We were born here."

"Why, I wasn't at all! You know that."

"Well, if you weren't, you couldn't help it. You got here early. You were very little when I first saw you with your mother. Cécile, every autumn, before I start for the woods, I have a mass said at the *paroisse* in Ville-Marie for madame your mother."

Cécile pressed his hand softly and drew closer to him. Whenever Charron spoke of her mother, or of his own, his voice lost its tone of banter; he became respectful, serious, simple. It was clear enough that for him the family was the first and final thing in the human lot; and it was so engrafted with religion that he could only say:

"Very well; religion for the fireside, freedom for the woods."

As they passed the end of the long Seminary building, the door of the garden stood open, and within they saw Bishop Laval, walking up and down the sanded paths, his breviary open in his hand. It was a very small garden; a grass plot in the centre, a row of Lombardy poplars along the wall, some lilac bushes, now in bloom, a wooden seat with no back under a crooked quince-tree. The old man caught sight of Pierre, though he walked so noiselessly,—beckoned to him and called out his name. The Bishop knew everyone along the river so well that it was said he could recognize a lost child by the family look in its face.

Pierre snatched off his cap and they went inside the garden door. Monseigneur inquired after the health of Madame Charron, and of the aged nun Marguerite Bourgeoys. And had Pierre heard whether Mademoiselle Le Ber was in health?

Not directly. He supposed she was as usual; he had heard nothing to the contrary.

The Bishop breathed heavily, like a tired horse. "All the sinners of Ville-Marie may yet be saved by the prayers of that devoted girl," he said with a certain meaning in his tone. "And you, my son, have you been to your confessor since your return from the woods?"

Pierre said respectfully that he had. The Bishop then turned to Cécile and placed his hand upon her head, with the rare smile which always seemed a little sad on his grim features.

"And here we have a child who borrows money,—and of a poor priest, too! Why did you never come to pay me back my twenty sous?"

"But Monseigneur l'Ancien, I gave them to Houssart, the very day after!"

"I know you did, my child, but I should have liked it better if you had come to me when you paid your debt. You are not afraid of me?"

"Oh, no, Monseigneur! But you are always occupied, and I did not know whether you liked to have children come."

"I do. I like it very much. Make me a visit here in my garden some morning at this hour, and I will share my lilacs with you; they are coming on now. Bring the little boy, if you like. I hear from the Pommiers that you and your father are making a good boy of him, and that is very commendable in you."

During the rest of the short walk to the cobbler's, Pierre asked what the Bishop meant by the twenty sous, but he seemed to pay little attention to the story; he was rather overcast, indeed. It was not until he greeted Madame Pommier that he recovered his high spirits.

II

For Charron, that evening, the apothecary brought up from his cellar some fiery Bordeaux, proper for a son of Languedoc, and the hours flew by. After Cécile had said good-night and gone upstairs to her summer bed-room, the two men talked on until after midnight; of the woods, of the state of the fur trade, of the results of the Count's last Indian campaign, and the ingratitude of the King, who had rewarded his services so inadequately.

Pierre lost his reserve after a bottle or two of fine Gaillac, and the conversation presently took a very personal turn. Auclair, in speaking of Madame Charron's illness, remarked that it was fortunate she had such nurses at hand as the Sisters of the Congregation.

"Oh, yes, they took good care of her, to be sure," Pierre admitted. "And why not? By Heaven, they owe me something, those women! Fifty thousand gold écus, perhaps!"

"Charron," said his host reprovingly, "you do yourself wrong to pretend that you are chagrined at having lost that dowry. You are not a mean-spirited man. You have never cared much about money."

"Perhaps not, but I care about defeat. If the venerable Bourgeoys had not got hold of that girl in her childhood and overstrained her with fasts and penances, she would be a happy mother today, not sleeping in a stone cell like a prisoner. There are plenty of girls, ugly, poor, stupid, awkward, who are made for such a life. It was bad enough when she was shut up in her father's house; but now she is no better than dead. Worse."

"Still, if it is the life she desires, and if her father can bear it—"

"Oh, her father, poor man! I do not like to meet him on the street,—and he does not like to meet me. I recall to him the days when she first came home from Quebec and used to be at her mother's side, at the head of a long table full of good company, always looking out for everyone, saying the right thing to everyone. It did his eyes good to look at her. He was never the same man after she shut herself away. I was in his employ then, and I know. He used to talk to me and say: 'It is like a fever; it will burn itself out in time. We shall all be happy again.' This went on three years, and he was always hoping. But not I. I saw her before I broke away to the woods, though. I made sure."

Pierre took out a pouch of strong Indian tobacco, pulverized it in his brown palm, and put it into his pipe. He drew the smoke in deep, like a man overwrought. Auclair had meant to bring out some old brandy to flavour their talk, but he thought: "No, better not." Aloud he said:

"You mean that you had an interview with Mademoiselle Le Ber after she went into retreat?"

"Call it an interview. I made sure." Charron took the pipe out of his mouth and spoke rapidly. "It was in the fourth year of her retreat. I had lost hope, but I wanted to know. She always went out of the house to early mass. One morning in the spring, when it gets light early, I went to the narrow allée between her garden and the church and waited there under an apple-tree that hung over the wall. When she came along with her old servant, I stepped out in front of her and spoke. Ah, that was a beautiful moment for me! She had not changed. She did not shrink away from me or reproach me. She was gracious and gentle, as always, and at her ease. She put back her grey veil as we talked, and looked me in the eyes. There was still colour in her cheeks,—not rosy as she used to be, but her face was fresh and soft, like the apple blossoms on that tree where we stood. She had no hard word for me. She said she was glad of a chance to see me again and to bid me farewell; she meant to re-new her vows when the five years were over, and we should never meet again. When I began to cry,—I was young then,—and knelt down before her, she put her hand on my head; she did not fear me or the few people who hurried past us into the church,—they seemed frightened enough at such a sight, but she was calm. She told me it would be better if I left her father, and that I must marry. *I will always pray for you*, she said, *and when you have children, I will pray for them. As long as we are both in this world, you may know I pray for you every day; that God may preserve you from sudden death without repentance, and that we may meet in heaven.*"

Charron sat silent for a moment, then bent over the candle and lit his pipe, which had gone out. "You know, monsieur, three times in the woods my comrades have thought it was all over with me; a powder explosion, my canoe going down under me in the rapids, and then the gunshot wound I had in the Count's last campaign. I have remembered that promise; for I have certainly been delivered from sudden death. I remember, too, her voice when she said those words,—it was still her own voice, which made people love to go to her father's house, and one felt gay if she but spoke one's name. And now it is harsh and hollow like an old crow's—terrible to hear!"

Auclair began to wonder whether Pierre might have had anything to drink before he came to dinner. "Now you are talking wildly, my boy. We cannot know what her voice is like now."

"I know," said Charron sullenly. He crossed the room to the door of the enclosed staircase, and examined it to see that it was shut. "The little one cannot hear, up there? No?" He sat down and leaned forward, his elbows on the table. "I know. I have heard her. I have seen her."

"Pierre, you have not done anything irreverent, that the nuns will never forgive?" Auclair was alarmed by the very thought that the sad solitaire, who asked for nothing on this earth but solitude, had perhaps been startled.

Charron was too much excited and too sorry for himself at that moment to notice his friend's apprehensions.

"It was like this," he went on presently. "You know, because of my mother, this year I got back to Montreal early, months before my time. There is not much to do there, God knows, except to be a pig, and I never behave like dirt in my mother's town. We live so near the chapel of the Congregation that I can never get the recluse out of my mind. You remember there were two weeks of terrible cold in March, and it made me wretched to think of her walled up there. No, don't misunderstand me!" Charron's eyes came back from their far-away point of vision and fixed intently, distrustfully, on his friend's face. "All that is over; one does not love a woman who has been dead for nearly twenty years. But there is such a thing as kindness; one wouldn't like to think of a dog that had been one's playfellow, much less a little girl, suffering from cold those bitter nights. You see, there are all those early memories; one cannot get another set; one has but those." Pierre's voice choked, because something had come out by chance, thus, that he had never said to himself before. The candles blurred before Auclair a little, too. God was a witness, he murmured, that he knew the truth of Pierre's remark only too well.

After he had relit his pipe and smoked a little, Charron continued. "You know she goes into the church to pray before the altar at midnight. Well, I hid myself in the church and saw her. It is not difficult for a man who has

lived among the Indians; you slide into the chapel when
an old sacristan is locking up after vespers, and stay there
behind a pillar as long as you choose. It was a long wait.
I had my fur jacket on and a flask of brandy in my pocket,
and I needed both. God's Name, is there any place so cold
as churches? I had to move about to keep from aching all
over,—but, of course, I made no noise. There was only
the sanctuary lamp burning, until the moon came round
and threw some light in at the windows. I knew when it
must be near midnight, you get to have a sense of time
in the woods. I hid myself behind a pillar at the back of
the church. I felt a little nervous, sorry I had come, perhaps.—At last I heard a latch lift,—you could have heard
a rabbit breathe in that place. The iron grille beside the
altar began to move outward. She came in, carrying a
candle. She wore a grey gown, and a black scarf on her
head, but no veil. The candle shone up into her face. It
was like a stone face; it had been through every sorrow."

Charron stopped and crossed himself. He shut his eyes
and dropped his head in his hands. "My friend, I could
remember a face!—I could remember Jeanne in her little
white furs, when I used to pull her on my sled. Jacques
Le Ber would have burned Montreal down to keep her
warm. He meant to give her every joy in the world, and
she has thrown the world away. . . . She put down her
candle and went toward the high altar. She walked very
slowly, with great dignity. At first she prayed aloud,
but I scarcely understood her. My mind was confused;

her voice was so changed,—hoarse, hollow, with the sound of despair in it. Why is she unhappy, I ask you? She is, I know it! When she prayed in silence, such sighs broke from her. And once a groan, such as I have never heard; such despair—such resignation and despair! It froze everything in me. I felt that I would never be the same man again. I only wanted to die and forget that I had ever hoped for anything in this world.

"After she had bowed herself for the last time, she took up her candle and walked toward that door, standing open. I lost my head and betrayed myself. I was well hidden, but she heard me sob.

"She was not startled. She stood still, with her hand on the latch of the grille, and turned her head, half-facing me. After a moment she spoke.

"*Poor sinner*, she said, *poor sinner, whoever you are, may God have mercy upon you! I will pray for you. And do you pray for me also.*

"She walked on and shut the grille behind her. I turned the key in the church door and let myself out. No man was ever more miserable than I was that night."

III

Ever since Cécile could remember, she had longed to go over to the Île d'Orléans. It was only about four miles down the river, and from the slopes of Cap Diamant she could watch its fields and pastures come alive in the spring, and the bare trees change from purple-grey to green. Down the middle of the island ran a wooded ridge, like a backbone, and here and there along its flanks were cleared spaces, cultivated ground where the islanders raised wheat and rye. Seen from the high points of Quebec, the island landscape looked as if it had been arranged to please the eye,—full of folds and wrinkles like a crumpled table-cloth, with little fields twinkling above the dark tree-tops. The climate was said to be more salubrious than that of Quebec, and the soil richer. All the best vegetables and garden fruits in the market came from the Île, and the wild strawberries of which Cécile's father was so fond. Giorgio, the drummer boy, had often told her how well the farmers lived over there; and about the great eel-fishings in the autumn, when the islanders went out at night with torches and seined eels by the thousand.

Pierre Charron had a friend on the island, Jean Baptiste Harnois, the smith of Saint-Laurent, and he meant to go over and pay him a visit this summer, before he went back to Montreal. He had promised to take Cécile along,—every time he came to the shop, he reminded her that they were to make this excursion. One fine morning in the last week of June he dropped in to say that the wind was right, and he would start for the island in about an hour, to be gone for three days.

Very well, Auclair told him, Cécile would be ready.

"But three days, father!" she exclaimed; "can you manage for yourself so long? You bought so many things at the market for me to cook."

"I can manage. You must go by all means. You may not have such a chance again."

"Good," said Pierre. "I will be back in an hour. And she must bring a warm coat; it will be cold out on the water."

Cécile had never gone on a voyage before,—had never slept a night away from home, except during the Phips bombardment, when she and her mother had taken refuge at the Ursuline convent, along with the other women and children from the Lower Town.

"What shall I take with me, Father? I am so distracted I cannot think!"

"The little valise that was your mother's will hold your things. You will need a night-gown, and a pair of stockings, and a clean cotton blouse, and some handkerchiefs; I should think that would be all. And I will give you a package of raisins as a present for Madame Harnois."

She ran upstairs and began to pack her mother's bag, finding it hard to assemble her few things in her excitement.

"Are you ready, Cécile?" her father presently called from the foot of the stairs.

"I am not sure, Father—I think so. I wish I had known yesterday."

"Then you would not have slept all night. Come along, and I will put the raisins in your valise."

Pierre was waiting, seated on the long table that served

as a counter. Her father looked into her bag to see that she had the proper things, then handed it to him. Cécile put on her cap and coat. Auclair kissed her and wished them *bon voyage*. "Take good care of her, Pierre."

Pierre touched his hand to his black forelock. "As you would yourself, monsieur." He pushed Cécile out of the door before him.

"Papa," she called back, "you will not forget to keep the fire under the soup? It has been on only an hour."

Pierre's boat was a light shallop with one sail. He rowed out far enough to catch the breeze and then sat in the stern, letting the wind and current carry them. He had made a change in his clothes during the hour he was absent from the shop, Cécile noticed (later in the day she wondered why!), had put on a white linen shirt and knotted a new red silk neckerchief about his throat. He soon took off his knitted cap, lit his pipe, and lounged at his ease. On one shore stretched the dark forest, on the other the smiling, sunny fields that ran toward Beaupré. Behind them the Lower Town grew smaller and smaller; the rock of Kebec lost its detail until they could see only Cap Diamant, and the Château, and the spires of the churches. The sunlight on the river made a silver glare all about the boat, and from the water itself came a deep rhythmic sound, like something breathing.

"Think of it, Pierre, in all these years I have never been on the river before!" Such a stretch of lost opportunity as life seemed just then!

Pierre smiled. "Not so many years, at that! Your father is over-cautious, maybe, but squalls come up suddenly on this river, and most of these young fellows had as lief drown as not. I'd rather you never went with anyone but me. If you like it, you can go with me any time."

"But I'd like to go the other way,—to Montreal, and up those rivers that are full of rapids. I want to go as far as Michilimackinac."

"Some time, perhaps. We'll see how you like roughing it."

Cécile asked what he had in the stone jug she saw in the bow, along with his blanket and buckskin coat.

"That is brandy, for the smith. But it will come back full of good country wine. He makes it from wild grapes. The wild grapes on the island are the best in Canada; Jacques Cartier named it the Île de Bacchus because he found such fine grapes growing in the woods. That ought to please you, with all your Latin!"

"Are you like Mother Juschereau, do you think it wrong for a girl to know Latin?"

"Not if she can cook a hare or a partridge as well as Mademoiselle Auclair! She may read all the Latin she pleases. But I expect you won't like the food at the Harnois', *à la campagnarde*, you know,—they cook everything in grease. As for me, it doesn't matter. When you can go to an Indian feast and eat dogs boiled with blueberries, you can eat anything."

Cécile shuddered. "I don't see how you can do it, Pierre. I should think it would be easier to starve."

"Oh, do you, my dear? Try starving once; it's a long business. I've known the time when dog meat cooked in a dirty pot seemed delicious! But the worst food I ever swallowed was what they call *tripe de roche*. I went out to Lac la Mort with some Frenchmen early in the spring once. They were a green lot, and they let most of our provisions get stolen on the way. As soon as we reached the lake, we were caught in a second winter; a heavy snow, and everything frozen. No game, no fish. We had to fall back on *tripe de roche*. It's a kind of moss that grows on the rocks along the lake, something like a sponge; the cold doesn't kill it, when everything else is frozen hard as iron. You gather it and boil it, and it's not so bad as it goes down,—tastes like any boiled weed. But afterwards—oh, what a stomach-ache! The men sat round tied up in a knot. We had about a week of that stuff. We scraped the hair off our bear skins and roasted them, that time. But it's a truth, monkey, I wouldn't like a country where things were too soft. I like a cold winter, and a hot summer. My father used to boast that in Languedoc you were never out of sight of a field or a vineyard. That would mean people everywhere around you, always watching you! No hunting,—they put you in jail if you shoot a partridge. Even the fish in the streams belong to somebody. I'd be in prison in a week there."

The settlement at Saint-Laurent was Pierre's destination. After he had passed the point at Saint-Pétronille and turned into the south channel, a sweet, warm odour blew out from the shore, very like the smell of ripe strawberries. Each time the boat passed a little cove, this fragrance grew stronger, the air seemed saturated with it. All the early explorers wrote with much feeling about these balmy odours that blew out from the Canadian shores,—nothing else seemed to stir their imagination so much. That fragrance is really the aromatic breath of spruce and pine, given out under the hot sun of noonday, but the early navigators believed it was the smell of luscious unknown fruits, wafted out to sea.

When Pierre had made a landing and tied his boat, they went up the path to the smith's house, to find the family at dinner. They were warmly received and seated at the dinner-table. The smith had no son, but four little girls. After dinner Cécile went off into the fields with them to pick wild strawberries. She had never seen so many wild flowers before. The daisies were drifted like snow in the tall meadow grass, and all the marshy hollows were thatched over with buttercups, so clean and shining, their yellow so fresh and unvarying, that it seemed as if they must all have been born that morning at the same hour. The clumps of blue and purple iris growing in these islands of buttercups made a sight almost too wonderful. All the afternoon Cécile thought she was in paradise.

The little girls did not bother her much. They were

timid with a guest from town and talked very little. Two of them had been to Quebec, and even to her father's shop, and they asked her about the stuffed baby alligator, where it came from. They wanted to know, too, why her father bought so many pigs' bladders in the market. Did he eat them, or did he fill them with sausage meat? Cécile explained that he washed and dried them, and when people were sick, he filled the bladders with hot water and put them on the sore place, to ease the pain.

The little girls wore moccasins, but no stockings, and their brown legs were badly marked by brier scratches and mosquito bites. When they showed her the pigs and geese and tame rabbits, they kept telling her about peculiarities of animal behaviour which she thought it better taste to ignore. They called things by very unattractive names, too. Cécile was not at all sure that she liked these children with pale eyes and hay-coloured hair and furtive ways.

At supper she was glad to see Pierre and the genial blacksmith again, but the kitchen where they ate was very hot and close, for Madame Harnois shut all the doors and windows to keep out the mosquitos. There were mosquitos at home, on Mountain Hill, too, but her father drove them away by making a smudge of eucalyptus balls, which were sent to him from France every year.

The family went to bed early, and after darkness had shut off the country about them, and bedtime was approaching, Cécile felt uneasy and afraid of something. Pierre had brought his own blanket, and said he would sleep in the hayloft. She wished she could follow him, and with a sinking heart heard him go whistling across the wagon-yard.

There were only three rooms in this house, the kitchen and two bedrooms. In one of these slept the smith and his wife. In the other was a wide, low bed made of split poles, and there slept all the four daughters. There, Cécile soon gathered, she too must sleep! The mother told them to give Cécile the outside place in the bed, for manners. Slowly she undressed and put on her night-gown. The little Harnois girls took off their frocks and tumbled into bed in their chemises,—they told her they only wore night-gowns in winter. When they kicked off their moccasins, they did not stop to wash their legs, which were splashed with the mud of the marsh and bloody from mosquito bites. One candle did not give much light, but Cécile saw that they must have gone to bed unwashed for many nights in these same sheets. The case on the bolster, too, was rumpled and dirty. She felt that she could not possibly lie down in that bed. She made one pretext after another to delay the terrible moment; the children asked whether she said so many prayers every night. At last the mother called that it was time to put out the candle. She blew it out and crept into the bed, spreading a handkerchief from her valise down on the bolster-cover where she must put her head.

She lay still and stiff on the very edge of the feather bed, until the children were asleep and she could hear the smith and his wife snoring in the next room. His snore was only occasional, deep and guttural; but his wife's was high and nasal, and constant. Cécile got up very softly and dressed carefully in the dark. There was only one window in the room, and that was shut tight to keep out mosquitos. She sat down beside it and watched the moon come up,— the same moon that was shining down on the rock of Kebec. Perhaps her father was taking his walk on Cap Diamant, and was looking up the river at the Île d'Orléans and thinking of her. She began to cry quietly. She thought a great deal about her mother, too, that night; how her mother had always made everything at home beautiful, just as here everything about cooking, eating, sleeping, living, seemed repulsive. The longest voyage on the ocean could scarcely take one to conditions more different. Her mother used to reckon Madame Pigeon a careless housekeeper; but Madame Pigeon's easy-going ways had not prepared one for anything like this. She tried to think about the buttercups in the marsh, as clean as the sun itself, and the long hay-grass with the star-white daisies.

Cécile sat there until morning, through the endless hours until daylight came, careful never to look back at the rumpled bed behind her. When Madame Harnois stuck her head in at the door to waken her children, she complimented Cécile upon being up so early. All the family washed in a wooden basin which stood on a bench in the kitchen, and they all wiped their faces on the same towel. The mother got breakfast in her night-cap because she had not taken time to arrange her hair. Cécile did not want much breakfast; the bread had so much lard in it that she could not eat it. She had sagamite and milk.

When they got up from the table, Pierre announced that he was going fishing, and he did not even suggest taking her along. The little girls were expected to help their mother in the morning, so Cécile got away unobserved into the nearest wood. She went through it, and climbed toward the ridge in the middle of the island. At last she came out on a waving green hayfield with a beautiful harp-shaped elm growing in the middle of it. The grass there was much taller than the daisies, so that they looked like white flowers seen through a driving grey-green rain. Cécile ran across the field to that symmetrical tree and lay down in the dark, cloud-shaped shadow it threw on the waving grass. The tight feeling in her chest relaxed. She felt she had escaped for ever from the Harnois and their way of living. She went to sleep and slept a long while. When she wakened up in the sweet-smelling grass, with the grasshoppers jumping over her white blouse, she felt rested and happy,—though unreal, indeed, as if she were someone else. She was thinking she need not go back to the smith's house at all that day, but could lunch on wild strawberries, when she heard the little girls' voices calling her, "Cé-cile, Cé--cile!" rather mournfully, and she remembered that she ought not to cause the family anxiety. She looked for a last time at the elm-tree and the sunny field, and then started back through the wood. She didn't want the children to come to that place in their search for her. She hoped they had never been there!

After dinner she escaped into the fields again, but this time the girls went with her. They had a grape-vine swing in the wood; as she had never had a swing when she was little, she found it delightful. These children were nicer when they played at games and did not stand staring at one.

But as the sunlight began to grow intensely gold on the tree-tops and the slanting fields, dread and emptiness awoke in Cécile's breast again, a chilling fear of the night. The mother had found her handkerchief spread out on the bolster and had put on a clean bolster-slip. But that made little difference. She couldn't possibly lie in that bed all night, not even if the children had taken a bath before they got into it. As soon as they were asleep, she got up and sat by the window as on the first night.

At breakfast Pierre Charron noticed that Cécile did not look at all like herself. When they left the table, he asked her to go down to the spring with him, and as soon as they were alone, inquired if she were not feeling well.

"No, I don't feel well, and truly I can't stay here any longer. Please, please, Pierre, take me home today!"

Pierre had never seen her cry before, and he was greatly surprised. "Very good. There is not much wind, and perhaps we had better go today, anyhow. Get your things, and I'll tell the smith I've changed my mind."

Cécile ran swiftly back to the house. She knew she had not been a very satisfactory visitor, and she felt remorseful. She gave the little girls all the handkerchiefs she had brought with her,—they hadn't any, but wiped their sweaty faces on their sleeves or their skirts. Several of her handkerchiefs had come from her aunts, and she was very fond of them, but she parted with them gladly and only wished she had more things to give the children.

She could scarcely believe in her good fortune when Pierre's boat actually left the shore and he began pulling out into the river, while the Harnois children stood waving to them from the cove.

"We needn't hurry, eh?" Pierre asked.

"Oh, no! I love being on the river," she replied unsteadily. He asked no further questions, but handled his oars, singing softly to himself. Of course, she thought sadly, he would never want to take her anywhere again. She used to dream that one day he might take her to Montreal in his boat, perhaps even to see the great falls at Niagara.

As soon as they were out of the south channel and had cleared the point of the island, they could see the rock of Kebec and the glare of the sun on the slate roofs. Cécile began to struggle with her tears again. It was as if she were home already. For a long while it did not grow much plainer; then it rose higher and higher against the sky.

"Now I can see the Château, and the Récollet spire," she cried. "And, oh, Pierre, there is the Seminary!"

"Yes? It's a fine building, but I never had any particular affection for it." He saw that she was much too happy to notice his banter.

Soon they could see the spire of Notre Dame de la Victoire—and then they were in the shadow of the rock itself. When she stepped upon the shore, Cécile remembered how Sister Catherine de Saint-Augustin, when she landed with her companions, had knelt down and kissed the earth. Had she been alone, she would have loved to do just that. They went hand in hand up La Place street, across the market square, down Notre Dame street beside the church, and into Mountain Hill. It was wonderful that everything should be just the same, when she had been away so long! Pierre did not bother her with questions, but she knew he was watching her closely. She was ashamed, but it couldn't be helped; some things are stronger than shame.

When they burst in upon her father, he was seated at his desk, rolling pills on a sheet of glass.

"What, back already?" He did not seem so overjoyed as Cécile had thought he would be.

"Yes, monsieur," Pierre replied carelessly, "we were a little bored in the country, both of us."

How grateful she was for that "*tous les deux*!" She might have known Pierre would not betray her.

"Father," she said as she kissed him again, "please ask Pierre Charron to come to dinner tonight. I want to make something very nice for him. I've given him a lot of trouble."

After Pierre was gone, and she had peeped into the salon and the kitchen to see that everything was as she had left it, Cécile came back into the shop.

"Father, Pierre took it on himself, but it was my fault we came home. I didn't like country life very well. I was not happy."

"But aren't they kind people, the Harnois? Haven't they kind ways?"

"Yes, they have." She sighed and put her hand to her forehead, trying to think. They had kind ways, those poor Harnois, but that was not enough; one had to have kind things about one, too. . . .

But if she was to make a good dinner for Pierre, she had no time to think about the Harnois. She put on her apron and made a survey of the supplies in the cellar and kitchen. As she began handling her own things again, it all seemed a little different,—as if she had grown at least two years older in the two nights she had been away. She did not feel like a little girl, doing what she had been taught to do. She was accustomed to think that she did all these things so carefully to please her father, and to carry out her mother's wishes. Now she realized that she did them for herself, quite as much. Dogs cooked with blueberries—poor Madame Harnois' dishes were not much better! These coppers, big and little, these brooms and clouts and brushes, were tools; and with them one made, not shoes or cabinet-work, but life itself. One made a climate within a climate; one made the days,—the complexion, the special flavour, the special happiness of each day as it passed; one made life.

Suddenly her father came into the kitchen. "Cécile, why did you not call me to make the fire? And do you need a fire so early?"

"I must have hot water, Papa. It is no trouble to make a fire." She wiped her hands and threw her arms about him. "Oh, Father, I think our house is so beautiful!"

BOOK V
THE SHIPS FROM FRANCE

THE SHIPS FROM FRANCE

I

At four o'clock in the morning Cécile was sitting by her upstairs window, dressed and wide awake. Across the river there was already a red and purple glow above the black pines; but overhead spread the dark night sky, like a tent with its flap up, letting in a new day,—the most important day of the year.

Word had come down by land that five ships from France had passed Tadousac and were beating up the river against head winds. During the night the wind had changed; Cécile had only to hold her handkerchief outside her window and watch it flutter, to reassure herself that a strong breeze was blowing in from the east, and the ships would be in today. She wondered how her father could go on sleeping. Nicholas Pigeon and Blinker had been up all night, making a great deal of noise as they turned out one baking after another to feed the hungry sailors. The smell of fresh bread was everywhere, very tempting to one who had been awake so long.

At last she heard a door below open softly, and she ran down the stairs to the salon and out into the kitchen, where her father was just beginning to make his fire.

"Oh, Father, the wind is right! I knew it would come! Yesterday all the nuns at the Ursulines' were praying for the wind to change. How soon do you suppose they will get in? You remember last year it rained all day when the first ships came. But today will be beautiful. I expect Kebec will look very fine to them."

"No better than they will to us, certainly. But there is no hurry. They will not be along for hours yet."

Cécile told him she had been awake nearly all night and was very hungry, so would he please hurry the chocolate. She herself ran out through the board fence that divided their back yard from the Pigeons', to get a loaf from Blinker, as it was not nearly time for the baker's boy to come on his rounds.

They had just sat down to their breakfast when they heard the front door open, and heavy, rapid little steps crossed the bare floor of the shop. Jacques came in, his pale eyes so round that he looked almost frightened.

"Hurry, Cécile, they're coming!" he called. Then, re-membering where he was, he snatched off his cap and murmured: "Pardon, monsieur. Bonjour, monsieur. Bonjour, Cécile."

Cécile sprang up. "You mean they are in sight, Jacques?"

"People say they are, nearly," he answered vaguely.

"What nonsense, Cécile! You are as foolish as the little boy. You know the cannon would be sounding and the whole town shouting if the ships were in sight. Sit down and calm yourselves, both of you. Jacques, here is some chocolate for you."

"Thank you, monsieur." He sat down on the edge of the chair and took the cup carefully in both hands, at the same time glancing at the clock. "But we must not be late," he added fearfully.

"We shall not be. The ships cannot possibly pass this end of the island before noon."

"Which ones do you think they will be, monsieur?"

"They will probably be old friends, that have come to us often before."

Jacques means he hopes one of them will be *La Garonne*, with the nice sailor who made our beaver," Cécile explained.

Jacques blushed and looked up at her trustfully. But his anxiety was too strong for him. In a few moments he stole another glance at the clock and resolutely put down his cup.

"If you please, monsieur, I think I will go now."

Auclair laughed. "You may both go! You are as restless

as kittens. I can do nothing with either of you about. I will follow you in an hour or two. You will have a long wait."

The children agreed they wouldn't mind that, and they ran out into the early sunshine and down the hill hand in hand.

"Oh, look at the market square, Jacques, look! I have never seen so many carts before."

Since long before daybreak the country people had been coming into town, bringing all they could carry in their carts and on their backs; fresh pork, dressed rabbits and poultry, butter and eggs, salad, green beans, leeks, peas, cucumbers, wild strawberries, maple sugar, spruce beer. The sailors, after two or three months on salt meat and ship's bread, would sell their very ear-rings for poultry and green vegetables. All the market-women, and the men, too, were dressed in their best, in whatever was left of the holiday costume they used to wear at home, in their native town. A sailor would always make straight for the head-dress or bonnet or jacket of his own *pays*.

The children found there was already a crowd at the waterside, and while they ran about, hunting for an advantageous post of observation, people kept streaming down Mountain Hill. The whole of the Upper Town was emptying itself into the Lower. The old people, who almost never left the house, came with the rest, and babies at the breast were carried along because there was no one at home to leave them with. Not even on great feast-days did one see so many people come together. Bishop Laval and his *donné* came down the hill and took their places in the crowd. Giorgio, the drummer boy, and Picard, the Count's valet, were sitting on one of the cannon that guarded the landing-place. Noël Pommier and his friend the wagon-maker came carrying old Madame Pommier between them, and a boy followed bringing her chair. There were even new faces: a company of Montreal merchants, who had been staying at the Château for several days, awaiting the ships.

All the poor and miserable were on the water front, as well as the great. 'Toinette was moving about in the crowd, looking fresh and handsome in a clean dress and a new kerchief. Her partner, the snail, with her hair curled very tight and her hands hidden under her apron, was standing among the poor folk over by the King's warehouse. Jacques was careful to keep out of his mother's way; but she had no wish to be bothered with him and was blind to his presence in the crowd. The Count did not come down the hill, but he was in plain view on the terrace in front of the Château, and with him were the Intendant and Madame de Champigny, and a group of officers with their wives. Everyone in Kebec, Cécile believed, except the cloistered nuns, was out today. Even Monseigneur de Saint-Vallier, though he was so proud, had a chair placed in the highest part of his garden and sat there looking down over the roofs, watching for the ships.

The hours dragged on. Babies began to cry and old

people to murmur, but nobody went away. Giorgio and Picard made a place for Jacques between them on the cannon. By the time her father arrived, Cécile was beginning to wonder whether she could possibly stand any longer. But very soon a shout went up—something flashed in the south channel against the green fields of the Île d'Orléans. Cécile held her breath and gripped her father's hand. It dipped, it rose again, a gleam of white. There could be no doubt now; larger and larger, the canvas of sails set full, with the wind well behind them. Soon the whole rigging rose above the rapidly dropping shore, then the full figure of a square-rigged ship emerged, passed the point of the island, and glided into the broad, undivided river. The cannon on the redoubt boomed the Governor's salute, and all the watchers on the waterside shouted a great welcoming cry, waving their caps, kerchiefs, aprons, anything at hand. Women, and men, too, cried for joy. Cécile hid her face on her father's shoulder, and Jacques stood up on the cannon, waving his little cap.

"*Les Deux Frères, Les Deux Frères!*" people began to shout, while others laughed at them. She was not near enough for anyone to be sure, but the townspeople knew those carrying boats by heart, held their lines and shape in mind all year. Sure enough, as the vessel bore up the river toward the rock, everyone agreed that it was *Les Deux Frères*, from Le Havre. Her anchor-chains had scarcely begun to rattle when the sound was drowned by new shouts; a second set of sails was sighted between the green fields and the pine-clad shore.

"*Le Profond, Le Profond!*" the people cried, and again the ordnance thundered from the redoubt.

Within half an hour the Captain of *Les Deux Frères* came ashore in a little boat, bringing dispatches for the Governor. But before he could make his way up to the Château, he had to stop to greet old friends and to answer the questions of the crowd that pressed about him.

The King was well, and Monsieur le Dauphin was in good health. The young Duc de Bourgogne—the King's grandson—was married to a little Princess of Savoie, only twelve years old, *mais bien sage*. The war was at a standstill; but of that they would hear later,—he tapped his dispatch-case. The wheat-harvest had been good last year, the vintage one of the best within memory. Of the voyage he had no time to speak; they had got here, hadn't they? That was the important thing.

The Captain made his way up the hill, and Bishop Laval went into the church of Notre Dame de la Victoire to thank God for preserving the King's health.

Sometimes, owing to bad weather and high winds, the ships of the first fleet came in four or five days apart; but this year they came in close succession. By sunset five vessels were anchored in the roadstead before Quebec: *Les Deux Frères, Le Profond, La Reine du Nord, La Licorne, Le Faucon.* They stood almost in a row, out in the river. Worn, battered old travellers they looked. It brought tears to the eyes to think how faithful they were, and how much they had endured and overcome in the years they had been beating back and forth between Canada and the Old World. What adverse winds those sails had been trimmed to, what mountains of waves had beaten the sides of those old hulls, what a wilderness of hostile, never-resting water those bows had driven through! Beaten southward, beaten backward, out of their course for days and even weeks together; rolling helpless, with sails furled, water over them and under them,—but somehow wearing through. On bad voyages they retraced their distance three and five times over, out-tiring the elements by their patience, and then drove forward again— toward Kebec. Sometimes they went south of Newfoundland to enter the Gulf, sometimes they came south of Labrador and through the straits of Belle Île; always making for this rock in the St. Lawrence. Cécile wondered how they could ever find it,—a goal so tiny, out of an approach so vast.

Many a time a boat came in wracked and broken, and it took all summer to make repairs, before the captain dared face the sea again. And all summer the hardships and mischances of the fleet were told over and over in Quebec. The greater part of the citizens had made that voyage at least once, and they knew what a North Atlantic crossing meant: little wooden boats matched against the immensity and brutality of the sea; the strength that came out of flesh and blood and goodwill, doing its uttermost against cold, unspending eternity. The colonists loved the very shapes of those old ships. Here they were again, in the roadstead, sending off the post-bags. And tomorrow they would give out of their insides food, wine, cloth, medicines, tools, fire-arms, prayer-books, vestments, altars for the missions, everything to comfort the body and the soul.

II

The next few days were like a continual festival, with sailors overrunning the town, and drinking and singing in the Place half the night. Every day was market day, and both Blinker and his master worked double shifts, trying to bake bread enough for five crews. The waterside was heaped with merchandise and casks of wine. The merchants employed every idle man and boy to help them store their goods, and all the soldiers were detailed to receive the supplies for the Château and the forts. Even the churches and the priests were busier than usual. The sailors, though they might indulge in godless behaviour, were pious in their own way; went to confession soon after they got into port, and attended mass. They lived too near the next world not to wish to stand well with it. Nobody begrudged them their rough pleasures; they never stole, and they seldom quarrelled. Even the strictest people, like Bishop Laval, recognized that men who were wet and cold and poorly fed for months together, who had to climb the rigging in the teeth of the freezing gales that blew down from Labrador, must be allowed a certain licence during the few weeks they were on shore. The colony owed its life to these fellows; whatever else they did, they got the ships to Quebec every year.

Cécile was allowed to take Jacques for an escort and go down to the waterside in the morning to watch the unloading,—until the third day, when Auclair's own goods, from the old drug house in the parish of Saint-Paul, were brought ashore from *Le Profond*. In a few hours the orderly shop, and the salon behind it, were full of bales and boxes. M. Auclair said they must begin unpacking at once, as with this confusion there was no room for customers to come and go. Jacques had followed the carriers up the hill, and he decided that he would rather stay and see these boxes opened than share in the general excitement on the waterside.

The apothecary took off his coat and set to work with his hammer and chisel. Blinker, very curious to see everything that came out of the boxes, ran in between bakings to carry the lumber and straw down into the cellar. One by one the white jars on the shelves, and the drawers of the cabinets, were filled up again; with powders, salts, gums, blue crystals, strong-smelling spices, bay-leaves, lime flowers, camomile flowers, senna, hyssop, mustard, dried plants and roots in great variety. There was the usual crate of small wooden boxes containing fruits conserved in sugar, very costly and much prized in Quebec. These boxes could not be opened, of course, as they were the most expensive articles in Auclair's stock, but it delighted the children to read the names on the covers: figs, apricots, cherries, candied lemon rind, and crystallized ginger.

While Cécile and Jacques were counting over these boxes of sweetmeats and wondering who would buy such luxuries, Auclair told them he was much more interested in a jar labelled "*Bitumen—oleum terræ*" than in the conserves. It contained a dark, ill-smelling paste which looked like wagon grease; a kind of petroleum jelly that seeped out of the rocks in a certain cairn on the island of Barbados and was carried from thence to France. He had great need for it here in Canada; he purified it, added a small amount of alcohol and borax, and prepared a remedy for snow-blindness, with which hunters and trap pers and missionaries were so cruelly afflicted in winter. So far, no cure had been discovered that gave such relief. A physician in Montreal had tried a similar treatment, using goose grease and lard instead of the *oleum terræ*, with very bad results. This, Auclair explained to the children, was because all animal fat contained impurities, and this "Barbados tar," as it was vulgarly called, might be regarded as a mineral fat. He went on to say that in general he distrusted remedies made of the blood or organs of animals, though he must admit that some were of exceptional value. For a hundred years and more the

Breton fishermen, who went as far as Newfoundland and Labrador for their catch, had been making a medicinal oil from the fat livers of the codfish, and had an almost fanatical faith in its benefits. He himself had used it in Quebec for cases of general decline, and found it strengthening.

"But I detest all medicines made from lizards and serpents," he concluded his lecture, "even viper broth."

"Viper broth, Father? I have never heard of that. Is it an Indian medicine?"

"My dear, at the time when we came out to Canada, it was very much the fashion at home. Half the great ladies of France were drinking a broth made from freshly killed vipers every morning, instead of their milk or chocolate, and believed themselves much the better for it. Medicine is a dark science, as I have told you more than once."

"Yes, but everything here in our shop is good for people. We know that, don't we, Jacques? You shouldn't speak against medicines, Father, when our new ones have just come and we are feeling so happy to have them. You always worry, you know, when any of the jars are nearly empty."

"Oh, we do what we can, my dear! We can but try." Her father took up his chisel again and began to pry the lid from another box. "The perplexing thing is that honest pharmaciens get such different results from the same remedy. Your grandfather, all his life, believed that he had helped many cases of epilepsy with powdered unicorn's horn, which he got from Africa at great expense; while I have so low an opinion of it that I never keep it in my shop."

"But your cough-sirops, Papa, both kinds, help everyone. And Madame Renaude says she could never milk her cows in the morning if she did not put your rheumatism ointment on her hands at night."

Auclair laughed. "You are your mother over again. No matter on whom I tried a new remedy, she was always the first to feel its good effects. But what is this, Cécile? A package addressed to you, and in Aunt Blanche's handwriting, here among my Arabian spices! Why, she must have taken it to the pharmacie and persuaded Monsieur Neuillant to pack it with his drugs, to ensure quick delivery. Now we shall have something of whose goodness there can be no doubt. No, you must open it yourself. Jacques and I will look on."

Night-gowns, with yokes beautifully embroidered by Aunt Blanche herself; a pair of stockings knit by the little cousin Cécile; a woollen dressing-gown; two jerseys, one red and one blue; a blue silk dress, all trimmed with velvet bands, to wear to mass; a gold brooch and a string of coral beads from Aunt Clothilde. Cécile unfolded them one after another and held them up to view. Never had a box from home brought such fine things before. What did it mean?

"It means that you are growing up now and must soon dress like a young lady. The aunts bear that fact in mind,

—more than I, perhaps." Auclair sighed and became thoughtful.

Jacques clasped his two hands together and looked up at Cécile with his slow, utterly trustful and self-forgetful smile.

"Oh, Cécile," he breathed, "you will look so beautiful!"

III

Pierre Charron had come down from Montreal and was giving a supper party for his friend Maître Pondaven, captain of *Le Faucon*. Cécile and her father were the only guests invited, though Pierre had said they might bring Jacques along to see the Captain's parrot. It was to be a party in the open air, down by the waterside, under the full moon.

Cécile had no looking-glass upstairs—the only one in the house was in the salon—so she always dressed by feeling rather than by sight. This afternoon she put on the blue silk dress with black velvet bands, walked about in it, then took it off and spread it out on her bed, where she smoothed it and admired it. It was too different from anything she had ever worn before, too long and too grand —quite right to wear to mass or to a wedding, perhaps, but not for tonight. She slipped on one of her new jerseys and felt like herself again. The coral beads she would wear; they seemed appropriate for a sailor's party. She left the beautiful dress lying on her bed and went down to see that her father had brushed his Sunday coat, and to give Jacques's hands a scrubbing. She and the little boy sat down on the sofa to wait for Pierre, while Auclair was arranging his shop for the night. To Cécile the time dragged very slowly. She was thinking, not about the novelty of having supper by moonlight, or of the *tête de veau* they were promised, or of the celebrated Captain Pondaven, but of his parrot.

All her life she had longed to possess a parrot. The idea of a talking bird was fascinating to her—seemed to belong with especially rare and wonderful things, like orange-trees and peacocks and gold crowns and the Count's glass fruit. Her mother, she whispered to Jacques, had often told her about a parrot kept in one of the great houses at home, which saw a servant steal silver spoons and told the master. Then there was the imprisoned princess who taught her parrot to say her lover's name, and her cruel brothers cut out the bird's tongue. Magpies were also taught to speak, but they could say only a word or two.

At last she heard Pierre's voice at the front door.

"All ready, Monsieur Euclide?"

Cécile jumped up from the sofa and ran into the shop.

"We have been ready a long while, Pierre. I thought you had forgotten us."

"Little stupid!" Pierre pinched her ear.

Auclair now looked at his daughter for the first time.

"But I supposed you would wear the new dress from Aunt Blanche?"

Cécile coloured a little. "I feel better like this. You don't mind, Pierre Charron?"

"Not a bit! This is a picnic, not a dinner of ceremony. Monsieur Auclair, will you be kind enough to bring some of those little nuts you burn to keep off mosquitoes?"

"Ah yes, the eucalyptus balls! Certainly, that is a good idea. I will fill my pockets." The apothecary put on the large beaver hat which he wore only to weddings and funerals, and they set off down the hill, the two men before, Cécile and Jacques following.

Down on the water-front, at some distance behind the church of Notre Dame de la Victoire, a row of temporary cabins were put up each summer, where hot food was served to the sailors on shore leave. In one of these Renaude-le-lièvre, the butter-woman, and an old dame from Dinan sold fresh milk and butter and Breton pancakes to the seamen from that part of the world. Tonight they had prepared a special supper for the Captain, of whom all the Bretons were proud; he had come up from a *mousse* and had made his own way in the world. Pierre had ordered things he knew the Captain liked; a dish made of three kinds of shell-fish, a *tête de veau*, which la Renaude did very well, a roast capon with a salad, and for dessert Breton pancakes with honey and preserves.

When the party arrived, their table was waiting for them, with a white cloth, and a lantern hung from a pole

—already lit, though it was not yet dark and a pale moon was shining in a clear evening sky. While Pierre was giving instructions to the cooks, Captain Pondaven was being rowed ashore by two of his crew. He came up from the landing, his parrot on his shoulder, dressed as no one there had ever seen him before, in his Breton holiday suit, which he carried about the world with him in his sailor's chest; a black jacket heavily embroidered in yellow, white knee-breeches, very full and pleated at the belt, black cloth leggings, and a broad-brimmed black hat with a shallow crown. He was a plain, simple man, direct in his dealings as in his glance, and he came from Saint-Malo, where the grey sea breaks against the town walls.

At first Cécile thought him a little sombre and solemn, but after a mug of Jamaica rum he was more at his ease, and as the supper went on he grew very companionable. She had hoped he would begin to tell at once about his voyages and the strange countries he had seen, but he seemed to wish to talk of nothing but his own town and his family. He had four boys, he said, and one little girl.

"And she is the only one who was born when I was at home. I am always a little anxious about her. The boys are strong like me and can take care of themselves, but she is more delicate,—not so sturdy as Mademoiselle here, though perhaps Mademoiselle is older."

"I was thirteen last month," Cécile told him.

"And she will be eleven in December. I am nearly always at home for her birthday."

Auclair asked him whether by home he meant Le Havre or Saint-Malo. The seaman looked surprised.

"Saint-Malo, naturally. I was born a Malouin."

"I know that. But since you take on your cargo at Le Havre, I thought you perhaps lived there now."

"Oh, no! One is best in one's own country. I run back to Saint-Malo after my last trip, and tie up there for the winter."

"But that must add to your difficulties, Monsieur Pondaven."

"It is nothing to me. I know the Channel like my own town. All my equipage are glad to get home. They are all Malouins. I should not know how to manage with men from another part."

"You Malouins stick together like Jesuits," Pierre declared. "Yet by your own account you were not so well treated there that you need love the place."

Captain Pondaven smiled an artless smile. "Perhaps that is the very reason! He means, Monsieur Auclair, that the town brought me up like a stepmother. My father was drowned, fishing off Newfoundland, and my mother died soon afterwards. With us, when an orphan boy is twelve years old, he is given a suit of clothes and a chest and is sent to sea as a *mousse*. They sent me out with a hard master my first voyage. But when I came back from Madagascar and showed how my ears were torn and my back was scarred, the townspeople took up my case and got my papers changed. My townspeople did not do so badly by me. When I was ready for a command, they saw that I had my chance. They put their money behind me, and I have been half-owner in my boat for five years now."

Though she liked the Captain very much and gave polite attention to his talk, Cécile's mind was on the parrot. He sat forgotten on the back of the chair, attached to his master's belt by a long cord. He seemed of a sullen disposition—there was nothing gay and bird-like about him. Neither was he so brilliant as she had expected. He was all grey, except for rose-coloured tail-feathers, and his plumage was ruffled and untidy, for he was moulting. He gave no sign of his peculiar talent, but sat as silent as the stuffed alligator at home, never moving except to cock his head on one side. When the leek soup put a temporary stop to conversation, she ventured a question.

"And what is your parrot's name, if you please, Monsieur Pondaven?"

The Captain looked up from his plate and smiled at her. "His name is Coco, mademoiselle, and he will make noise enough presently. He is a little shy with strangers, not seeing many on board."

Then the shell-fish came on, and Auclair asked the Captain what people at home thought of the King's peace with the English.

He said he did not know what the inland people thought. "But with us on the coast it will make little difference. The King cannot make peace on the sea. Our people will take an English ship whenever they have a chance. They are looking for good plunder this summer. We must have our revenge for the ships they took from us last year."

"They are fine seamen, the English," Pierre Charron declared. Cécile had noticed that he was in one of his perverse moods, when he liked to tease and antagonize everyone a little.

The Captain answered him mildly. "Yes, they are good sailors, but we usually get the better of them. They are a blasphemous lot and have no respect for good manners or religion. That never pays."

Auclair reminded him that last summer the English had captured one of the boats bound for Canada.

"I remember well, *Le Saint-Antoine*, and the Captain is a friend of mine. They took the boat into Plymouth and sold her at auction. Many of our merchants lost heavily. Your Bishop, Monseigneur de Saint-Vallier, had sent some things for the missions over here by *Le Saint-Antoine*. Some bones of the saints and other holy relics were packed in an oak chest, and the Captain, out of respect, put it in his own cabin. The English, when they plundered the ship, came upon this chest and supposed it was treasure. When they opened it, they were furious. After committing every possible sacrilege they took the relics to the cook's galley and threw them into the stove where their dinner was cooking."

Cécile asked whether no punishment had come upon those sailors.

"Not at the time, mademoiselle, but I shouldn't like to put to sea with such actions on my soul,—and I am no coward, either."

"*Sales cochons anglais, sales cochons!*" said another voice, and she realized that at last the parrot had spoken. Jacques put his hand over his mouth to stifle a cry. Pierre and her father laughed, and applauded the parrot, but Cécile was much too startled to laugh. She had supposed that the speech of parrots called for a good deal of imagination on the part of the listener, like the first efforts of babies. But nobody could possibly mistake what this bird said. Had he been out of sight, in the shed kitchen with Mère Renaude, she would have thought some queer old person was in there, talking in a vindictive tone.

"Oh, monsieur, isn't he wonderful!" she gasped.

The Captain was pleased. "You find him amusing? Yes, he is a clever bird; you will see. Now let us all clink our cups together,—you, too, little man,—and perhaps he will say something else."

They rattled their pewter mugs several times, and the bird came out with: "*Vive le Roi, vive le Roi!*" Jacques began jumping up and down with excitement.

"He is a loyal subject of the King," said Pondaven. "He has been taught to say that when the cups clink.

But for the most part, I don't teach him; he picks up what he likes."

"And do you always take him to sea with you, monsieur?"

"Nearly always, mademoiselle. My men believe he brings us good luck; they like to have him on board. I have his cage swung in my cabin, and when the ship pitches badly, I tie it down."

"But how does he endure the cold?" Auclair asked. "These are tropical birds, after all."

"Yes, his brother died of a chill on his first voyage— I had two of them. But this one seems to stand it. When he begins to shiver, I give him a little brandy in warm water —he is very fond of it—and I put a blanket over him. He will live to be a hundred if I can keep him from taking cold."

Conscious that he was the centre of attention, the parrot began to croon softly: "*Bon petit Coco, bon petit Coco. Ici, ici!*"

Jacques and Cécile left their places and stood behind the Captain's chair to watch the bird's throat. Pondaven explained that he was an African parrot, and that was why he had so many tones of voice, harsh and gentle, for the African birds have a much more sensitive ear than the West Indian.

"Should you like to hear him whistle a tune, mademoiselle? He can, if he will. We will try to have a little concert." He put the parrot on his knee, took a piece of maple sugar from the table, and held it before the un-blinking yellow eyes. Then the Captain began to whistle a song of his own country:

> *A Saint-Malo, beau port de mer,*
> *Trois gros navires sont arrivés.*

After a few moments the bird repeated the air perfectly —his whistle was very musical, sounded somewhat like a flute. He was given the sugar, and stood on one foot while he fed himself with the other. The company now became interested in the *tête de veau*, but Jacques and Cécile scarcely tasted the dish for watching Coco. They were both wishing they could carry him off and keep him in the apothecary shop for ever.

"Has Coco a soul, Cécile?" Jacques whispered.

"I wonder! I will ask the Captain after a while, but we must listen now."

Captain Pondaven was relating some of the wonderful happenings in his own town. Presently he told them the story of how a great she-ape, brought to Saint-Malo as a curiosity by the Indian fleet, had one day broken her chain and run about the town. She dashed into a house, snatched a baby from its cradle, and ran up to the house-tops with it,—and in Saint-Malo, he reminded them, the houses are four and even five storeys high. While all the terrified neighbours gathered in the street, the mother fell on her knees, shut her eyes, and appealed to the Blessed Virgin. The ape clambered along the roofs until she came to a house where an image of Our Lady stood in a little alcove up under the eaves. Into this recess the beast thrust the baby, and left it there, as safe as if it were with its own mother.

The children and the apothecary thought this a charming story, but Pierre sniffed. "Oh, you have nothing over us in the way of miracles!" he told the Captain. "Here we have them all the time. Every Friday the beaver is changed into a fish, so that good Catholics may eat him without sin. And why do you look at me like that, Mademoiselle Cécile?"

"Everyone knows he is not changed, Pierre. He is only considered as a fish by the Church, so that hunters off in the woods can have something to eat on Fridays."

"And suppose in Montreal some Friday I were to consider a roast capon as a fish? I should be put into the stocks, likely enough!"

Captain Pondaven smiled and shook his head. "Mademoiselle has the better of you, Charron. A man can make fun of the angels, if he sets out to. But I was going to tell the little boy here that in our town, when a child is naughty, we still tell him the she-ape will get him; and the children are as much afraid of that beast as if she were alive."

The time had come for story-telling; Pondaven and Pierre Charron began to entertain each other with tales of the sea and forest, as they always did when they got together.

At about ten o'clock Father Hector Saint-Cyr came out from the Château, where he had been to lay before Count Frontenac a petition from the Christianized Indians of his mission at the Sault. He lingered on the terrace to enjoy the prospect,—he got to Quebec but seldom. The moon was high in the heavens, shining down upon the rock, with its orchards and gardens and silvery steeples. The dark forest and the distant mountains were palely visible. This was not the warm white moonlight of his own Provence, certainly, which made the roads between the mulberry-trees look like rivers of new milk. This was the moonlight of the north, cold, blue, and melancholy. It threw a shimmer over the land, but never lay in velvet folds on any wall or tower or wheat-field. Out in the river the five ships from France rode at anchor. Some sailors down in the Place were singing, and when they finished, their mates on board answered them with another song.

Why, the priest wondered, were these fellows always glad to get back to Kebec? Why did they come at all? Why should this particular cliff in the wilderness be echoing tonight with French songs, answering to the French tongue? He recalled certain naked islands in the Gulf of the St. Lawrence; mere ledges of rock standing up a little out of the sea, where the sea birds came every year to lay their eggs and rear their young in the caves and hollows; where they screamed and flocked together and made a clamour, while the winds howled around them, and the spray beat over them. This headland was scarcely more than that; a crag where for some reason human beings built themselves nests in the rock, and held fast.

Down yonder by the waterside, before one of the rustic booths, he could see a little party seated about a table with lanterns. He could not see who they were, but he felt a friendliness for that company. A little group of Frenchmen, three thousand miles from home, making the best of things,—having a good dinner. He decided to go down and join them.

IV

The apothecary, in his shirt-sleeves, was standing on a wooden bench, taking down from the shelves of a high cabinet large sheets of paper, to which dried plants were attached by narrow strips of muslin gummed down with gum Arabic. This was his herbarium, his collection of medicinal Canadian plants which he meant to take back to France. Cécile, busily knitting, had been watching him for a long while. When at last he got down and began assorting the piles of paper, she spoke to him.

"Papa, what will become of Jacques when we go back to France?"

Her father was engaged with a plant of the milkweed kind, which the French colonists called *le cotonnier*. He did not look up.

"Ah, my dear, I have the Count's perplexities and my own,—I cannot arrange a future for your little protégé."

"But, Father, how can we leave him, with no one to look after him? I shall always be thinking of him, and it will make me very unhappy."

"You will soon have your little cousins for companions; Cécile, and André, and Rachel. Cousin André will fill Jacques's place in your heart."

"No, Papa. My heart is not like that."

She spoke quickly, almost defiantly, in a tone she had never used to her father before. He did not notice it; he was trying to decide which of two gentians was the better preserved. For a month now he had been distracted and absent-minded. Cécile went quietly into the salon. She almost hated that little André who was so fortunate, who had a wise and charming mother to watch over him, a father to provide for him, and a rich aunt to give him presents. Laying aside her knitting, she put on her cap and went out to walk about the town.

This was the first week of October. The autumn had been warm and sunny,—but rather sad, as always. After the gay summer, came the departures. First Pierre Charron had gone back to Montreal. Then Captain Pondaven, who had been coming to the apothecary shop so often that he seemed like a familiar friend, had suddenly set sail for his old town where the grey sea beat under the castellated walls. Three new ships had come in during September: *La Garonne, Le Duc de Bretagne, Le Soleil d'Afrique.*

But *La Garonne* did not bring the Breton sailor Jacques waited for, and his mates reported that he had shipped on a boat in the West India trade.

None of the ships brought the word Cécile's father and the Governor were so impatiently expecting. A dark spirit of discontent and restlessness seemed to be sitting in the little salon behind the shop. All peace and security had departed. The very furniture looked ill at ease, as if it did not believe in its own usefulness any more. Perhaps the sofa and the table and the curtains had overheard her father say that he could not take them home with him, but must leave them to be scattered among the neighbours. Cécile wished that she could be left and scattered, too. She stayed out of doors and away from the house as much as possible. Her father cared little about his dinner now—sometimes forgot to go to market. So why should she spend the golden afternoons indoors?

The glorious transmutation of autumn had come on: all the vast Canadian shores were clothed with a splendour never seen in France; to which all the pageants of all the kings were as a taper to the sun. Even the ragged cliff-side behind her kitchen door was beautiful; the wild cherry and sumach and the blackberry vines had turned crimson, and the birch and poplar saplings were yellow. Up by Blinker's cave there was a mountain ash, loaded with orange berries.

In the Upper Town the grey slate roofs and steeples were framed and encrusted with gold. A slope of roof or a dormer window looked out from the twisted russet branches of an elm, just as old mirrors were framed in gilt garlands. A sharp gable rose out of a soft drift of tarnished foliage like a piece of agate set in fine gold-smith's work. So many kinds of gold, all gleaming in the soft, hyacinth-coloured haze of autumn: wan, sickly gold of the willows, already dropping; bright gold of the birches, copper gold of the beeches. Most beautiful of all was the tarnished gold of the elms, with a little brown in it, a little bronze, a little blue, even—a blue like amethyst, which made them melt into the azure haze with a kind of happiness, a harmony of mood that filled the air with content. The spirit of peace, that acceptance of fate, which used to dwell in the pharmacy on Mountain Hill, had left it and come abroad to dwell in the orchards and gardens, in the little stony streets where the leaves blew about. Day after day Cécile had walked about those streets trying to capture that lost content and take it home again. She felt almost as if she no longer had a home; often wished she could follow the squirrels into their holes and hide away with them for the winter.

This afternoon she saw that her father scarcely cared at all for those they would leave behind,—the only friends she had ever known. She was miserable, too, because she had spoken angrily to him. All the way up the hill her heart grew heavier, and the neat garden of the Récollets, where she was always welcome, seemed so full of sadness that she could not stay. She went into the Cathedral, found a dark corner behind the image of Saint Anthony, and knelt to pray. But she could only hide her face and cry. Once giving way to tears, she wept bitterly for all that she had lost, and all that she must lose so soon. Her mother had had the courage to leave everything she loved and to come out here with her father; she in turn ought to show just that same courage about going back, but she could not find it in her heart. "*O ma mère, je suis faible! Je n'ai pas l'esprit fort comme toi!*" she whispered under her sobs.

Bishop Laval, who was kneeling in the recess of a chapel, heard a sound of smothered weeping. He rose, turned about, and regarded her for some moments. Without saying a word he took her hand and led her out through the sacristy door into the garden of the Priests' House, where his poplar-trees were all yellow and the ground was covered with fallen leaves. He made her sit down beside him on a bench and waited until she had dried her tears.

"We are old friends, little daughter," he said kindly. "Your mother was a woman of exemplary piety. Have you been to your spiritual director with your troubles?"

"Oh, excuse me, Monseigneur l'Ancien! I am sorry to give way like this. I did not know it was coming on me."

"Can I help you in any way, my child?"

Cécile thought perhaps he could. At any rate, she felt a longing to confide in him. She had never been intimidated by his deep-set, burning eyes or his big nose. She always felt a kind of majesty in his grimness and poverty. Seventy-four years of age and much crippled by his infirmities, going about in a rusty old cassock, he yet commanded one's admiration in a way that the new Bishop, with all his personal elegance, did not. One believed in his consecration, in some special authority won from fasting and penances and prayer; it was in his face, in his shoulders, it was he.

Cécile turned to him and told him in a low voice how she and her father expected to leave Quebec very soon and go back to France, and how hard it would be for her to part from her friends. "And what troubles me most is the little boy, Jacques Gaux. You have been so kind as to ask about him sometimes, mon père, and perhaps after we are gone you will not forget him. I wish someone would bear him in mind and look after him a little."

"You must pray for him, my child. It is to such as he that our Blessed Mother comes nearest. You must unceasingly recommend him to her, and I will not forget to do so."

"I shall always pray for him," Cécile declared fervently, "but if only there were someone in this world, here in Quebec—Oh, Monseigneur l'Ancien," she turned to him pleadingly, "everyone says you are a father to your people, and no one needs a father so much as poor Jacques! If you would bid Houssart keep an eye on him, and when he sees the little boy dirty and neglected, to bring him here, where everything is good and clean, and wash his face! It would help him only to sit here with you—he is like that. Madame Pommier would look after him for me, but she cannot get about, and Jacques will not go to her, I am afraid. He is shy. When he is very dirty and ragged, he hides away."

"Compose yourself, my child. We can do something. Suppose I were to send him to the Brothers' school in Montreal, and prepare him for the Seminary?"

She shook her head despondently. "He could never learn Latin. He is not a clever child; but he is good. I don't think he would be happy in a school."

"Schools are not meant to make boys happy, Cécile, but to teach them to do without happiness."

"When he is older, perhaps, Monseigneur, but he is only seven."

"I was only nine when I was sent to La Flèche, and that is a severe school," said the Bishop. Perhaps some feeling of pity for his own hard boyhood, the long hours of study, the iron discipline, the fasts and vigils that kept youth pale, rose in his heart. He sighed heavily and murmured something under his breath, of which Cécile caught only the words: "... *domus* ... *Domine*."

She thanked him for his kindness and curtsied to take her leave. He walked with her to the garden door. "I will not forget what you have confided to my care, and I will seek out this child from time to time and see what can be done for him. But our Blessed Mother can do more for him than you or I. Never omit to present him to her compassion, my daughter."

Cécile went away comforted. Merely sitting beside the Bishop had given her an escape from her own thoughts. His nature was so strong of its kind, and different from that of anyone else she knew. She was hurrying home with fresh courage when she met Jacques himself, coming up the hill to look for her.

"I went to your house," he said, "but monsieur your father was occupied, so I came away."

"That was right. Have you had a bite of anything?"

He shook his head.

"Neither have I. If my father is busy with his plants, we should only bother him. Let us get a loaf from Monsieur Pigeon and take it up by the redoubt, and watch the sun go down."

By the time they had called at the baker's and climbed to the top of Cap Diamant, the sun, dropping with incredible quickness, had already disappeared. They sat down in the blue twilight to eat their bread and await the turbid afterglow which is peculiar to Quebec in autumn; the slow, rich, prolonged flowing-back of crimson across the sky, after the sun has sunk behind the dark ridges of the west. Because of the haze in the air the colour seems thick, like a heavy liquid, welling up wave after wave, a substance that throbs, rather than a light.

That crimson flow, that effulgence at the solemn twilight hour, often made Cécile think about the early times and the martyrs—coming up, as it did, out of those dark forests that had been the scene of their labours and their fate. The rainbow, she knew, was set in the heavens to remind us of a promise that all storms shall have an ending. Perhaps this afterglow, too, was ordained in the heavens for a reminder.

"Jacques," she said presently, "do you ever think about the martyrs? You ought to, because they were so brave."

"I don't like to think about them. It makes me feel bad," he murmured. He was sitting with his hands on his knees, looking vaguely into the west.

Cécile squeezed his arm. "Oh, it doesn't me! It makes me feel happy, as if I could never be afraid of anything again. I wish you and I could go very far up the river in Pierre Charron's canoe, and then off into the forests to the Huron country, and find the very places where the martyrs died. I would rather go out there than—anywhere." Rather than go home to France, she was thinking.

But perhaps, after she grew up, she could come back to Canada again, and do all those things she longed to do. Perhaps some day, after weeks at sea, she would find herself gliding along the shore of the Île d'Orléans and would see before her Kebec, just as she had left it; the grey roofs and spires smothered in autumn gold, with the Récollet flèche rising slender and pure against the evening, and the crimson afterglow welling up out of the forest like a glorious memory.

BOOK VI
THE DYING COUNT

BOOK SIX

THE DYING COUNT

I

Count Frontenac sat at the writing-table in his long room, driving his quill across sheets of paper. He was finishing a report to Pontchartrain, the Minister, which was to go by *Le Soleil d'Afrique*, sailing now in three days. Auclair stood by the fireplace, where the birch logs were smouldering,—it was now the end of October. He was remarking to himself that his master, often so put about by trifles, could bear with calmness a crushing disappointment.

All summer the Count had been waiting for his release from office, had confidently expected a letter summoning him to return to France to fill some post worthy of his past services.

When the King had sent him out here nine years ago,

it had been to save Canada—nothing less. The fur trade was completely demoralized, and the Iroquois were murdering French colonists in the very outskirts of Montreal. The Count had accomplished his task. He had chastised the Indians, restored peace and order, secured the safety of trade. He was now in his seventy-eighth year, and although he had repeatedly asked for his recall to France, the King had made no recognition of his services beyond sending him the Cross of St. Louis last autumn.

It was sometimes hinted that there was a personal reason for the King's neglect. There was an old story that because Madame de Montespan had been Count Frontenac's mistress before she became King Louis's, His Majesty disliked the sight of the Count. But Madame de Montespan had long ago fallen out of favour; she had been living in retirement for many years and never came to Court. The King himself was no longer young. Auclair doubted whether one old man would remember an affair of youthful gallantry against another old man,— when the woman herself was old and long forgotten.

He was thinking of this as he stood by the fire, awaiting his master's pleasure. At last the Governor pushed back his papers and turned to him.

"Euclide," he began, "I am afraid I cannot promise you much for the future. When the last ships came in, I had no doubt that I should go home on one of them,—and you and your daughter with me. By *La Vengeance* the Minister sends me a letter concerning the peace of Rijswijk, but ignores my petition for recall. He assures me of His Majesty's esteem, and of his desire to reward my services more substantially in the future. The future, for a man of my age, is an inconsiderable matter. His Majesty prefers that I shall die in Quebec."

The Count rose and walked to the window behind his desk, where he stood looking down at the ships anchored in the river, already loading for departure. As he stood there lost in reflection, Auclair thought he seemed more like a man revolving plans for a new struggle with fortune than one looking back upon a life of brilliant failures. The Count had the bearing of a fencer when he takes up the foil; from his shoulders to his heels there was intention and direction. His carriage was his unconscious idea of himself,—it was an armour he put on when he took off his night-cap in the morning, and he wore it all day, at early mass, at his desk, on the march, at the Council, at his dinner-table. Even his enemies relied upon his strength.

"I have never been a favourite," he said, turning round suddenly. "I have not the courtier's address. Without that, a military man cannot go far nowadays. Perhaps I offended His Majesty by trying to teach him geography. Nothing is more unpopular at Court than the geography of New France. They like to think of Quebec as isolated, French, and Catholic. The rest of the continent is a wilderness, and they prefer to disregard it. Any advance to the westward costs money—and Quebec has already cost them enough."

The Count returned to his desk, sat down, and went on talking in the impersonal, remote tone which he often adopted with his apothecary. Indeed, Auclair's chief service to his patron was not to administer drugs, but to listen occasionally, when the Governor felt lonely, to talk of places and persons,—talk which would have been incomprehensible to anyone else in Kebec.

"After my reappointment to Canada I had two audiences with His Majesty. The first was at Versailles, when he was full of a project to seize New York and the Atlantic seaports from the English. I was not averse to such an enterprize, but I explained some of the difficulties. With a small fleet and a few thousand regulars, I would gladly have undertaken it.

"My second audience was at Fontainebleau, shortly before we embarked from La Rochelle. The King received me very graciously in his cabinet, but he was no longer in a conqueror's mood; he had consulted the treasury. When I referred to the project he had advanced at our previous meeting, he glanced at the clock over his fireplace and remarked that it was the hour for feeding the carp. He asked me to accompany him. An invitation to attend His Majesty at the feeding of the carp is, of course, a compliment. We went out to the carp basins. I like a fine pond of carp myself, and those at Fontainebleau are probably the largest and fiercest in France. The pages brought baskets of bread, and His Majesty threw in the first loaves. The carp there are monsters, really. They came grunting and snorting like a thousand pigs. They piled up on each other in hills as high as the rim of the basin, with all their muzzles out; they caught a loaf and devoured it before it could touch the water. Not long before that, a care-taker's little girl fell into the pond, and the carp tore her to pieces while her father was running to the spot. Some of them are very old and have an individual renown. One old creature, red and rusty down to his belly, they call the Cardinal.

"Well, after the ravenous creatures had been fed by the royal hand, the King accompanied me a little way down the chestnut avenue. He wished me God-speed and said adieu. I took my departure by the great gate, where my carriage waited, and the King went back to the carp pond. That was my last interview with my royal master. That was the end of his bold project to snatch the seaports from the English and make this continent a French possession, as it should be. I sailed without troops, without money, to do what I could. Unfortunately for you, I brought you with me." The Count unlocked a drawer of his desk. He took out a leather bag and dropped it on his pile of correspondence. From its weight and the sound it made, Auclair judged it contained gold pieces.

"When I persuaded you to come out here," the Governor continued, "I promised you a return. I have already seen the captain of *Le Soleil d'Afrique* and bespoken his best cabin in case I have need of it. As you know, I am always poor, but in that sack there is enough for you to begin a modest business at home. If I were in your place, I should get my belongings together and embark the day after tomorrow."

"And you, Monsieur le Comte?"

"It is just possible that I may follow you next year. If not, Kebec is as near heaven as any place."

"Then I prefer to wait until next year also." Auclair spoke quietly, but without hesitation. "I came to share your fortunes."

The Governor frowned. "But you have your daughter's future to consider. At the present moment, I can in some degree assure you another start in the world. But if I terminate my days here, you will be adrift, and I doubt if you will ever get home at all. You are not very adept in practical matters, Euclide."

Auclair flushed faintly. "I have made my choice, patron. I remain in Kebec until you leave it. And I have no need for that," indicating the leather bag. "You pay me well for my services."

When the apothecary left the chamber, the Count looked after him with a shrug, and a smile in which there was both contempt and kindness. He remembered an incident very long ago: He had just come home from the foreign wars, and had nearly ruined himself providing a new coach and horses and liveries to make a suitable re-entrance in the world. The first time he went abroad in his new carriage, to pay calls in the fashionable part of Paris, the occupants of every coach he passed either were looking the other way, or saluted him carelessly, as if they had seen him only the day before. Not even a driver or a footman glanced twice at his fine horses. The gate-keepers and equerries at the houses where he stopped were insolently indifferent. Late in the afternoon, when he was crossing the Pont-Neuf at the crowded hour, in a stream of coaches, he saw among the foot-passengers the first admirers of his splendour: an old man and a young boy, gazing up and following his carriage with eager eyes— the grandfather and grandson who lived in the pharmacy next his stables and were his tenants.

II

The Count de Frontenac awoke suddenly out of a curious dream—a dream so vivid that he could not at once shake it off, but lay in the darkness behind his bed-curtains slowly realizing where he was. The sound of a church-bell rang out hoarse on the still air: yes, that would be the stubborn old man, Bishop Laval, ringing for early mass. He knew that bell like a voice. He was, then, in Canada, in the Château on the rock of Kebec; the St. Lawrence must be flowing seaward beneath his windows.

In his dream, too, he had been asleep and had suddenly awakened; awakened a little boy, in an old farm-house near Pontoise, where his nurse used to take him in the summer. He had been awakened by fright, a sense that some danger threatened him. He got up and in his bare feet stole to the door leading into the garden, which was ajar. Outside, in the darkness, stood a very tall man in a plumed hat and huge boots—a giant, in fact; the little boy's head did not come up to his boot-tops. He had no idea who the enormous man might be, but he knew that he must not come in, that everything depended upon his being kept out. Quickly and cleverly the little boy closed the door and slid the wooden bar,—he had no trouble in finding it, for he knew the house so well. But there was the front door,—he was sleeping in the wing of the cottage, and that front door was three rooms away. Still barefoot, he went softly and swiftly through the kitchen and the living-room to the hallway behind that main door, which could be fastened by an iron bolt. It was pitch-dark, but he did not fumble, he found the bolt at once. It was rusty, and stuck. He felt how small and weak his hands were—of that he was very conscious. But he turned the bolt gently back and forth in its hasp to loosen the rust-flakes, and coaxed it into the iron loop on the door-jamb which made it fast. Then he felt suddenly faint. He wiped the sweat from his face with the sleeve of his night-gown, and waited. That terrible man on the other side of the door; one could hear him moving about in the currant bushes, pulling at the rose-vines on the wall. There were other doors—and windows! Every nook and corner of the house flashed through his mind; but for the moment he was safe. The broad oak boards and the iron bolt were between him and the great boots that must not cross the threshold. While he stood gathering his strength, he awoke in another bed than the one he had quitted a few moments ago, but he was still covered with sweat and still frightened. He did not come fully to himself until he heard the call of the old Bishop's bell-clapper. Then he knew where he was.

Of all the houses he had slept in all over the world, in Flanders, Holland, Italy, Crete, why had he awakened in that one near Pontoise, and why had he remembered it so well? His bare feet had avoided every unevenness in the floor; in the dark he had stepped without hesitation from the earth floor of the kitchen, over the high sill, to the wooden floor of the living-room. He had known the exact position of all the furniture and had not stumbled against anything in his swift flight through the house. Yet he had not been in that house since he was eight years old. For four summers his nurse, Noémi, had taken him there. It was her property, but on her son's marriage the daughter-in-law had become mistress, according to custom. Noémi had taken care of him from the time he was weaned until he went to school. His own mother was a cold woman and had little affection for her children. Indeed, the Count reflected, as he lay behind his bed-curtains recovering from his dream, no woman, probably, had ever felt so much affection for him as old Noémi.

Not all women had found him so personally distasteful as his wife had done; but not one of his mistresses had felt more than a passing inclination for him. Tenderness, un-calculating, disinterested devotion, he had never known. It was in his stars that he was not to know it. Noémi had loved his fine strong little body, grieved when he was hurt, watched over him when he was sick, carried him in her arms when he was tired. Now, when he was sick indeed, his mind, in sleep, had gone back to that woman and her farm-house on the Oise.

It struck him that a dream of such peculiar vividness signified a change in himself. A change had been coming on all summer—during the last few months it had pro-gressed very fast. When from his windows he saw the last sail going out between the south shore and the Île d'Orléans, he knew he would never live to see those boats come back. Now, after this dream, he decided to make his will before another night fell.

Of late the physical sureness and sufficiency he had known all his life had changed to a sense of limitation and uncertainty. He had no wish to prolong this state. There was no one in this world whom he would be sorry to leave. His wife, Madame de la Grange Frontenac, he had no desire to see again, though he would will to her the little property he had, as was customary. Once a year she wrote him a long letter, telling him all the gossip of Paris and informing him of the changes which occurred there. From her accounts it appeared that the sons of most of his old friends had turned out badly enough. He could not feel any very deep regret that his own son had died in youth,—killed in an engagement in the Low Countries many years ago.

The Count himself was ready to die, and he would be glad to die here alone, without pretence and mockery, with no troop of expectant relatives about his bed. The world was not what he had thought it at twenty—or even at forty.

He would die here, in this room, and his spirit would go before God to be judged. He believed this, because he had been taught it in childhood, and because he knew there was something in himself and in other men that this world did not explain. Even the Indians had to make a story to account for something in their lives that did not come out of their appetites: conceptions of courage, duty, honour. The Indians had these, in their own fashion. These ideas came from some unknown source, and they were not the least part of life.

In spiritual matters the Count had always accepted the authority of the Church; in governmental and military matters he stoutly refused to recognize it. He had known absolute unbelievers, of course; one, a witty and blasphemous scapegrace, the young Baron de La Hontan, he had sheltered here in the Château, under the noses of two Bishops. But it was for his clever conversation, not for his opinions, that the Count offered La Hontan hospitality.

When the grey daylight began to sift through the hangings of his bed, Count Frontenac rang for Picard to bring his coffee.

"I shall not get up today, Picard," he remarked. "You may shave me in bed. Afterwards, go to the notary and fetch him here to transact some business with me. Stop at the apothecary shop on your way, and tell Monsieur Auclair I shall not need him until four o'clock."

When Auclair arrived in the afternoon, he found his patron still in bed, in his dressing-gown. To his inquiries the Count replied carelessly:

"Oh, I do very well indeed! I find myself so comfortable that I have almost decided to stay in bed for the rest of my life. I have been making my will today, and that reminded me of a promise I once gave your daughter. That bowl of glass fruit on the mantel: do not forget to take it to her when you go home tonight, with my greetings. She has always admired it. And there is another matter. In the leather chest in my dressing-room you will find a large package wrapped in brown Holland. It is table linen that I brought out from Île Savary. Tonight, when you will not be observed, I wish you to take it home with you for safe keeping. Upon Cécile's marriage, you will present it to her from me. Why do you look sober, Euclide? You know very well that I must soon change my climate, as the Indians say, and this Château will be in other hands. I merely arrange to dispose of my personal belongings as I wish."

"Monsieur le Comte, if you would permit me to try the remedy I suggested yesterday—"

"Tut-tut! We will have no more remedies. A little repose and comfort. The machine is worn out, certainly; but if we let it alone, it may go a little longer, from habit. When you come up tonight, you may bring me something to make me sleep, however. These long hours of wakefulness do a man no good. Draw up a chair and sit down by the fire, where I can speak to you without shouting. If you are to be in constant attendance here, you cannot be forever standing."

Picard was called to put more wood on the fire, and after he withdrew the Governor lay quiet for a time. The grey light of the rainy afternoon grew so pale that Auclair could no longer see his patient's face, and supposed he had fallen asleep. But suddenly he spoke.

"Euclide, do you know the church of Saint-Nicholas-des-Champs, out some distance?"

"Certainly, Monsieur le Comte. I remember it very well."

"Many of my family are buried there; a sister of whom I was fond. I shall be buried here, in the chapel of the Récollets, but I should like my heart to be sent back to France, in a box of lead or silver, and buried near my sister in Saint-Nicholas-des-Champs. I have left instructions to that effect in my will, but I prefer to tell you, as I suppose you will have to attend to it. That is all we need say on the subject.

"Monseigneur de Saint-Vallier called here today, but as I was engaged with the notary, he left word that he would make his visit of ceremony tomorrow. I should be pleased if some indisposition were to keep him at home. If he looks for any apologies or recantations from me, he will be disappointed. The old one will not bother me with civilities." Auclair heard the Count chuckle. "The old one knows where he stands, at least, and never bends his neck. All the same, a better man for this part of the world than the new one. Saint-Vallier belongs at the Court—where he came from."

The Count fell into reflection, and his apothecary sat silent, waiting for his dismissal. Both were thinking of a scene outside the windows, under the low November sky—but the river was not the St. Lawrence. They were looking out on the Pont-Marie, and the hay-barges tied up at the Port-au-Foin. On an afternoon like this the boatmen would be covering the hay-bales with tarpaulins, Auclair was thinking, and about this time the bells always rang from the Célestins' and the church of Saint-Paul.

When the fire fell apart and Auclair got up to mend it, the Count spoke again, as if he knew perfectly well what was in the apothecary's mind. "The Countess de Frontenac writes me that the Île Saint-Louis has become a very fashionable quarter. I can remember when it was hardly considered a respectable place to live in,—when they first began building there, indeed!"

"And my grandfather could remember when it was a wood-pile, patron; before the two islands were joined into one. He was never reconciled to the change, poor man. He always thought it the most convenient place for the wood-supply of our part of Paris."

III

One dark afternoon in November Cécile was sitting in the front shop, knitting a stocking. She sat in her own little chair, placed beside her father's tall stool, on which she had put a candle, as the daylight was so thick. Though the street outside was wet and the fog brown and the house so quiet, and though the Count was ill up in the Château, she was not feeling dull, but happy and contented. As she knitted and watched the shop, she kept singing over Captain Pondaven's old song, about the three ships that came

A Saint-Malo, beau port de mer,
Chargés d'avoin', chargés de bléd.

No more boats from France would come to Quebec as late as this, even her father admitted that, and his herbarium had been put back on the high shelves of the cabinet, where it belonged. As soon as those dried plants were out of sight, the house itself changed; everything seemed to draw closer together, to join hands, as it were. Cécile had polished the candlesticks and pewter cups, rubbed the table and the bed-posts and the chair-claws with oil, darned the rent in her father's counter-pane. A little more colour had come back into the carpet and the curtains, she thought. Perhaps that was only because the fire was lit in the salon every evening now, and things always looked better in the fire-light. But no, she really believed that everything in the house, the furni-ture, the china shepherd boy, the casseroles in the kitchen, knew that the herbarium had been restored to the high shelves and that the world was not going to be destroyed this winter.

A life without security, without plans, without prepa-ration for the future, had been terrible. Nothing had gone right this fall; her father had not put away any wood-doves in fat, or laid in winter vegetables, or bought his supply of wild rice from the Indians. "But we will manage," she sometimes whispered to her trusty poêle when she stuffed him with birch and pine.

Cécile tended the shop alone every afternoon now. A notice on the door requested messieurs les clients to be so good as to call in the morning, as the pharmacien was occupied elsewhere in the afternoon. Nevertheless clients came in the afternoon, especially country people, and her father placed all the most popular remedies on one shelf and marked them clearly, so that Cécile could dispense them when they were called for.

This afternoon, just as she was about to go for another candle, she thought she heard her father coming home;

but it proved to be Noël Pommier, the cobbler, who wanted a mixture of rhubarb and senna that M. Auclair sometimes made up for his mother.

Cécile sprang up and told him it was ready at hand, plainly marked. "*Et préféreriez-vous les pilules, ou le liquide, Monsieur Noël?*"

"*Les pilules, s'il vous plaît, mademoiselle. Et votre père?*"

"He is always at the Château after three o'clock. The Governor had been indisposed for two weeks now."

"Everyone knows that, mademoiselle," said the cobbler with a sigh. "Everyone is offering prayers for his recovery. It will be bad for all of us if anything goes wrong with the Count."

"Never fear, monsieur! My father is giving him every care, and he grows a little stronger each day."

"God grant it, mademoiselle. Picard is very much discouraged about his master. He says he cannot shave himself any more and does not look like himself. Picard thinks he ought to be bled."

"Oh, Monsieur Pommier, I wish you could hear what my father has to say to that! And what does Picard know about medicine? But he is not the only one. Other people have tried to persuade my father to bleed the Governor, but he is as firm as a rock."

"I have no doubt Monsieur Auclair knows best, Mademoiselle Cécile; but people will talk at such times, when a public man is ill."

Pommier had scarcely gone when her father came in, with a dragging step and a mournful countenance.

"Papa," said Cécile as she brought him his indoor coat, "I know you are tired, but the dinner will soon be ready. Sit down by the fire and rest a little. And, Father, won't you try to look a little more confident these days? The people watch you, and when you have a discouraged air, they all become discouraged."

"You think so?" He spoke anxiously.

"I am sure of it, Papa. I can tell by the things they say when they call here in your absence. You must look as if the Governor were much, much better."

"He is not. He is failing all the time." Her father sighed. "But you are right. We must put on a better face for the public."

Cécile kissed him and went into the kitchen. Just as she was moving the soup forward to heat, she heard a sharp knock at the shop door. Her father answered it, and Bishop de Saint-Vallier entered. Auclair hurriedly brought more candles into the shop and set a chair for his visitor. After preliminary civilities the Bishop came to the point.

"I have called, Monsieur Auclair, to inquire concerning the Governor's condition. Do you consider his illness mortal?"

"Not necessarily. If he were ten years younger, I should not consider it serious. However, he has great vitality and may very easily rally from this attack."

The Bishop frowned and stroked his narrow chin. He was clearly in some perplexity. "When I called upon the Comte de Frontenac some days ago, he stated that his recovery would be a matter of a week, at most. In short, he refused to consider his indisposition seriously, though to my eyes the mark of death was clearly upon him. Does he really believe he will recover?"

"Very probably. And that is a good state of mind for a sick man."

"Monsieur Auclair," Saint-Vallier spoke up sharply, "I feel that you evade me. Do you yourself believe that the Count will recover?"

"I must ask your indulgence, Monseigneur, but in a case like the Count's a medical adviser should not permit himself to believe in anything but recovery. His doubts would affect the patient. If the Count still has the vital force I have always found in him, he will recover. His organs are sound."

Saint-Vallier seemed to pay little heed to this reply. His eyes had been restlessly sweeping the room from floor to ceiling and now became fixed intently upon one point —on the stuffed alligator, as it happened. He began to speak rapidly, with gracious rise and fall of the voice, but in his most authoritative manner.

"If the Governor's illness is mortal, and he does not realize the fact, he should be brought to realize it. He has a great deal to put right with Heaven. He has used his authority and his influence here for worldly ends, rather than to strengthen the kingdom of God in Septentrional France!" For the first time he flashed a direct glance at the apothecary.

Auclair bowed respectfully. "Such matters are beyond me, Monseigneur. The Governor does not discuss his official business with me."

"But there is always open discussion of these things! Of the Governor's stand on the brandy traffic, for example, which is destroying our missions. I have denounced his policy openly from the pulpit, and on occasions when I noted that you were present in the church. You cannot be ignorant of it."

"Oh, upon that subject the Governor has also spoken publicly. Everyone knows that he considers it an unavoidable evil."

Saint-Vallier drew himself up in his chair and adopted an argumentative tone. "And why unavoidable? You doubtless refer to his proposition that the Indians will sell their furs only to such traders as will supply them with brandy?"

"Yes, Monseigneur; and since the English and Dutch traders give them all the brandy they want, and better prices for their skins as well, we must lose the fur trade altogether if we deny them brandy. And our colony exists by the fur trade alone."

"That is our unique opportunity, Monsieur l'apothicaire, to sacrifice our temporal interests for the glory of God, and impress by our noble example the Dutch and English."

"If Monseigneur thinks the Dutch traders can be touched by a noble example—" Auclair smiled and shook his head. "But these things are all beyond me. I know only what everyone knows,—though I have my own opinions."

"If the Count's illness is as serious as it seems to me, Monsieur Auclair, he should be given an opportunity to acknowledge his mistakes before the world as well as to Heaven. Such an admission might have a salutary influence upon the administration which will follow his. Since he relies upon you, it is your duty to apprise him of the gravity of his condition."

Auclair met Saint-Vallier's glittering, superficial glance and plausible tone rather bluntly.

"I shall do nothing to discourage my patient, Monseigneur, any more than I shall bleed him, as many good people urge me to do. The mind, too, has a kind of blood; in common speech we call it hope."

The Bishop flushed—his sanguine cheeks were apt to become more ruddy when he was crossed or annoyed. He rose and gathered the folds of his cloak about him. "It is time your patient dropped the stubborn mask he has worn so long, and began to realize that none of his enterprises will benefit him now but such as have furthered the interests of Christ's Church in this Province. I have seen him, and I believe he is facing eternity."

Auclair expressed himself as much honoured by the Bishop's visit and accompanied him to the door, holding it open that the light might guide him across the street to the steps of his episcopal Palace. When he returned to the salon, Cécile was bringing in the soup.

"I began to think Monseigneur de Saint-Vallier would never go, Papa. How people do bother us about everything since the Count is ill! I am glad we can keep them away from him, at least."

Her father sat down and took a few spoonfuls of soup. "Why, I find I am quite hungry!" he declared. "And when I came home, I did not think I could eat at all. For some reason, our neighbour's visit seems to have made me more cheerful."

"That is because you were so resolute with him, Father!"

He smiled at her between the candles.

"What restless eyes he has, Cécile; they run all over everything, like quicksilver when I spill it. He kept looking in again and again at your glass fruit, there on the mantel. Do you know, I believe he drew some conclusion from that; he has seen it at the Château, of course. These men who are trained at Court all become a little crafty; they learn to put two and two together. I have always believed that is why our patron never got advancement at Versailles: he is too downright."

IV

It was late afternoon, and Cécile was alone—as she was nearly always now. The Count had died last night. Today her father had gone to the Château to seal his heart up in a casket, so that it could be carried back to France according to his wish. It was already arranged that Father Joseph, Superior of the Récollets, should take the casket to Montreal, then to Fort Orange, and down the river to New York, where the English boats came and went all winter. On one of those boats he would go to England, cross over to France, and journey to Paris with the Count's heart, to bury it in the Montmort chapel at Saint-Nicholas-des-Champs.

Auclair had been gone all the afternoon, and Cécile knew that he would come home exhausted from sorrow, from his night of watching, and from the grim duty which had taken him today to the Count's death-chamber. Cécile regarded this rite with awe, but not with horror; autopsies, she knew, must be performed upon kings and queens and all great people after death. That was the custom. Her father would have the barber-surgeon to help him,—though they were not very good friends, because they disagreed about bleeding people. The barber complained that the meddlesome apothecary took the bread out of his mouth.

Many times that afternoon Cécile went out to the doorstep and looked up at the Château. A light snow was falling, and the sky was grey. It was very strange to look up at those windows in the south end, and to know that there was no friend, no protection there. She felt as if a strong roof over their heads had been swept away. She was not sure that they would even have a livelihood without the Count's patronage. Their sugar and salt and wine, and her father's Spanish snuff, had always come from the Count's storehouses. The colonists paid very little for their remedies; if they brought a basket of eggs, or a chicken, or a rabbit, they thought they were treating their medical man very handsomely. But what she most dreaded was her father's loneliness. He had lived under the Count's shadow. The Count was the reason for nearly everything he did,—for his being here at all.

About four o'clock, as the darkness began to close in, Cécile put more wood on the fire in the salon and set some milk to warm before it. There was very little to eat in the house. Her father had not been to market for a week. Running to the door every few minutes, she at last saw him coming down the hill, with his black bag full of deadly poisons. He looked grey and sick as she let him in. Before he threw his black bag into the cupboard, he took out of it a lead box, rudely soldered over. She looked at it solemnly.

"Yes," he said, "it is all we have left of him. Father Joseph will set out for France in two days. I am in charge of this box until it starts upon its journey."

He placed it in the cabinet where he kept his medical books, then went into the salon and sank down in his chair by the fire. Cécile knelt on the floor beside him, resting her arms upon his knee. He bent and leaned his cheek for a moment on her shingled brown hair.

"So it is over, my dear," he sighed softly. "It has lasted a lifetime, and now it is over. Since I was six years old, the Count has been my protector, and he was my father's before me. To my mother, and to your mother, he was always courteous and considerate. He belonged to the old order; he cherished those beneath him and rendered his duty to those above him, but flattered nobody, not the King himself. That time has gone by. I do not wish to outlive my time."

"But you wish to live on my account, don't you, Father? I do not belong to the old time. I have got to live on into a new time; and you are all I have in the world."

Her father went on sadly: "The Count and the old Bishop were both men of my own period, the kind we looked up to in my youth. Saint-Vallier and Monsieur de Champigny are of a different sort. Had I been able to choose my lot in the world, I would have chosen to be like my patron, for all his disappointments and sorrows; to be a soldier who fought for no gain but renown, merciful to the conquered, charitable to the poor, haughty to the rich and overbearing. Since I could not be such a man and was born in an apothecary shop, it was my good fortune to serve such a man and to be honoured by his confidence."

Cécile slipped quietly away to pour the warm milk into a cup, and with it she brought a glass of brandy. Her father drank them. He said he would want no dinner tonight, but that she must prepare something for herself. Without noticing whether she did so or not, he sat in a stupor of weariness, dreaming by the fire. The scene at the Château last night passed again before his eyes.

The Count had received the Sacrament in perfect consciousness at seven o'clock. Then he sank into a sleep which became a coma, and lay for three hours breathing painfully, with his eyes rolled back and only a streak of white showing between the half-open lids. A little after ten o'clock he suddenly came to himself and looked inquiringly at the group around his bed; there were two nursing Sisters from the Hôtel Dieu, the Intendant and Madame de Champigny, Hector de Callières, Auclair, and Father Joseph, the Récollets' Superior, who had heard the Count's confession and administered the last rites of the Church. The Count raised his eyebrows haughtily, as if to demand why his privacy was thus invaded. He looked from one face to another; in those faces he read something. He saw the nuns upon their knees, praying. He seemed to realize his new position in the world and what was now required of him. The challenge left his face,—a dignified calm succeeded it. Father Joseph held the crucifix to his lips. He kissed it. Then, very courteously, he made a gesture with his left hand, indicating that he wished every one to draw back from his bed.

"This I will do alone," his steady glance seemed to say. All drew back.

"Merci," he said distinctly. That was the last word he

spoke. While the group of watchers stood four or five feet away from the bed, wondering, they saw that his face had become altogether natural and lost all look of suffering. He breathed softly for a few moments, then breathed no more. One of the nuns held a feather to his lips. Madame de Champigny got a mirror and put it close to his mouth, but there was no cloud on it. Auclair laid his head down on his patron's chest; there all was still.

As Auclair was returning home after midnight, under the glitter of the hard bright northern stars, he felt for the first time wholly and entirely cut off from France; a helpless exile in a strange land. Not without reason, he told himself bitterly as he looked up at those stars, had the Latin poets insisted that thrice and four times blessed were those to whom it befell to die in the land of their fathers.

While Auclair sat by the fire thinking of these things, numb and broken, Cécile was lying on the sofa, wrapped up in the old shawl Madame Auclair had used so much after she became ill. She, too, was thinking of what they had lost. They would indeed have another winter in Quebec; but everything was changed almost as much as if they had gone away. That sense of a strong protector had counted in her life more than she had ever realized. To be sure, they had not called upon the Count's authority very often; but to know that they could appeal to him at any moment meant security, and gave them a definite place in their little world.

The hours went by. Her father did not speak or move, not even to fix the fire, which was very low. For once, Cécile herself had no wish to set things right. Let the fire burn out; what of it?

At last there came a knock at the door, not very loud, but insistent,—urgent, as it were. Auclair got up from his chair.

"Whoever it is, send him away. I can see no one to-night." He went into the kitchen and shut the door behind him.

Cécile was a little startled,—death made everything strange. She took a candle into the shop, set it down on the counter, and opened the door. Outside there, against the snow, was the outline of a man with a gun strapped on his back. She had thrown her arms around him before she could really see him,—the set of his shoulders told her who it was.

"Oh, Pierre, Pierre Charron!" She began to cry abandonedly, but from joy. Never in all her life had she felt anything so strong and so true, so real and so sure, as that quick embrace that smelled of tobacco and the pine-woods and the fresh snow.

"*Petite tête de garçon!*" he muttered running his hand over her head, which lay on his shoulder. "There, don't try to tell me. I know all about it. I started for Kebec as soon as I heard the Count was sinking. Today, on the river, I passed the messengers going to Montreal; they called the word to me. And your father?"

"I don't know what to do, Pierre. It is worse with him than when my mother died. There seems to be no hope for us."

"I understand," he stroked her soothingly. "I knew this would be a blow to him. I said to myself in Ville-Marie: 'I must be there when it happens.' I came as quickly as I could. Never did I paddle so fast. The breeze was against me, there was no chance of a sail. I had only a half-man to help me—Antoine Frichette, you remember? That poor fellow for whom your father made the belly-band. He did his best, but since his hurt he has no wind. I'm here at last, to be of any use I can. Command me." He had loosed the big kerchief from his neck, and now he gently wiped her cheeks dry with it. Turning her face about to the candlelight, he regarded it intently.

"I wish you would go to him, Pierre. He is in the kitchen."

He kissed her softly on the forehead, unslung his gun, and went out into the kitchen. He, too, closed the door behind him. In the few moments while she was left alone in the shop, Cécile opened the outer door again and looked up toward the Château. The falling snow and the darkness hid it from sight; but she had once more that feeling of security, as if the strong roof were over them again; over her and the shop and the salon and all her mother's things. For the first time she realized that her father loved Pierre for the same reason he had loved the

Count; both had the qualities he did not have himself, but which he most admired in other men.

When they came in from the kitchen, Charron had his arm over Auclair's shoulder.

"*Cécile*," he called, "*je n'ai pas de chance*. Evidently I am too late for supper, and I have not had a morsel since I broke camp before daybreak."

"Supper? But we have had no supper here tonight. We had no appetite. I will make some for you, at once. There is not much in the house, I am afraid; my father has not been to market. Smoked eels, perhaps?"

Charron made a grimace. "Detestable! Even I can do better than that. I shot a deer for our supper in the forest last night, and I brought a haunch along with me,—outside, in my bag. What else have you?"

"Not much." Cécile felt deeply mortified to confess this, though it was not her fault. "We have some wild rice left from last year, and there are some carrots. We always have preserves, and of course there is soup."

"Excellent; all that sounds very attractive to me at the moment. You attend to everything else, but by your leave I will cook the venison in my own way. It's enough for us all, and there will be good pickings left for Blinker."

When Charron went out to get his game-bag, Auclair whispered to his daughter: "Are we really so destitute, my child? Do the best you can for him. I will open a box of the conserves from France."

He now seemed very anxious about his dinner, and she

could not forbear a reproachful glance at the head of the house, who had been so neglectful of his duties.

"And you, Monsieur Euclide," said Pierre, when he came back with the haunch in his hand, "you ought to produce something rather special from your cellar for us."

"It shall be the best I have," declared his host.

The supper lasted until late. After the dessert the apothecary opened a bottle of heavy gold-coloured wine from the South.

"This," he said, "is a wine the Count liked after supper. His family was from the South, and his father always kept on hand wines that were brought up from Bordeaux and the Rhone vineyards. The Count inherited that taste." He sighed heavily.

"Euclide," said Charron, "tomorrow it may be you or I; that is the way to look at death. Not all the wine in the Château, not all the wines in the great cellars of France, could warm the Count's blood now. Let us cheer our hearts a little while we can. Good wine was put into the grapes by our Lord, for friends to enjoy together."

When it was almost midnight, the visitor said he was too tired to go hunt a lodging, and would gladly avail himself of the invitation, often extended, but never before accepted, of spending the night here and sleeping on the sofa in the salon.

Cécile, in her upstairs bedroom, turned to slumber with

the weight of doubt and loneliness melted away. Her last thoughts before she sank into forgetfulness were of a friend, devoted and fearless, here in the house with them, as if he were one of themselves. He had not a throne behind him, like the Count (it had been very far behind, indeed!), not the authority of a parchment and seal. But he had authority, and a power which came from knowledge of the country and its people; from knowledge, and from a kind of passion. His daring and his pride seemed to her even more splendid than Count Frontenac's.

EPILOGUE

On the seventeenth day of August 1713, fifteen years after the death of Count Frontenac, the streets of Quebec and the headland overlooking the St. Lawrence were thronged with people. By the waterside the Governor-General and Monsieur Vaudreuil, the Intendant, with all the clergy, regular and secular, the magistrates, and the officers from the garrison, stood waiting to receive a long-expected guest. Down the river lay a ship from France, *La Manon*, unable to come in against the wind. A small boat had been sent out to bring in one of her passengers. As the little boat drew near the shore, all the cannon on the fortifications, and the guns on the vessels anchored in the roadstead, thundered a salute of welcome to Monseigneur de Saint-Vallier, at last returning to his people after an absence of thirteen years.

When the prelate put foot upon the shore of Quebec, the church-bells began to ring, and continued to ring while the Governor-General, the Intendant, and the Archidiacre made addresses of welcome. The Intendant's carriage stood ready to convey the Bishop, but he preferred, characteristically, to ascend on foot to the Cathedral in the Upper Town, surrounded by the clergy and preceded by drums and hautbois.

Euclide Auclair, the old apothecary, standing before his door on Mountain Hill to watch the procession, was shocked at the change in Monseigneur de Saint-Vallier. When he sailed for France thirteen years ago, he was a very young man of forty-seven; now he came back a very old man of sixty. Every physical trait by which Auclair remembered the handsome and arrogant churchman had disappeared. He would never have recognized, in this heavy, stooped, lame old man going up the hill, the slender and rather dramatic figure he had so often seen mounting the steps of the episcopal Palace across the way. The narrow, restless shoulders were fat and bent; the Bishop carried his head like a man broken to the yoke.

Auclair watched the procession until the turn of the way shut Monseigneur de Saint-Vallier from sight, then went back to his shop and sat down, overcome. The thirteen years which for him had passed quietly, happily, had been bitter ones for the wandering Bishop. Nine years ago Saint-Vallier was on his way back to Canada after one of his long absences, when his ship, *La Seine*, was captured by the English, taken into London, and sold at auction. The Bishop himself was declared a prisoner of state, and was sequestered in a small English town near Farnham until the French King should ransom him.

Politics intervened: King Louis had lately seized and imprisoned the Baron of Méan, Dean of the Cathedral of Liége. The German Emperor was much offended at this, and besought Queen Anne not to release the Bishop of Quebec under any other terms than as an exchange for the Baron of Méan. For five years Saint-Vallier remained a prisoner of state in England, until King Louis at last set the Baron of Méan at liberty and recalled the Bishop of Quebec to France. But this did not mean that he was free to return to Canada. During his captivity his enemies in Quebec and Montreal had been busy, had repeatedly written the Minister, Pontchartrain, that the affairs of the colony went better with the Bishop away; that the King would be assisting his Canadian subjects by keeping Saint-Vallier in France. This the King did. He kept him, indeed, almost as long as the Queen of England had done.

That period of detention in France had sobered and saddened the wilful Bishop. His captivity in England he could ascribe to the hostilities of nations; to himself and to others he was able to put a very good face on it. But he could not pretend that he was kept in France for any other reason than that he was not wanted in Quebec. He had to admit to the Minister that he had made mistakes; that he had not taken the wise course with the Canadian colonists. Only by unceasing importunities, and by working upon the sympathies of Madame de Maintenon, who had always befriended him, had he ever wrung from the King permission to sail back to his diocese.

On this day of his return, even his enemies were softened at seeing how the man was changed. In place of his former assurance he seemed to wear a leaden mantle of humility; he climbed heavily up the hill to the Cathedral as if he were treading down the mistakes of the past.

Auclair, the apothecary, on the other hand, had scarcely changed at all. His delicate complexion had grown a trifle sallow from staying indoors so much, but the years which had made the Bishop an old man had passed lightly over the apothecary. Even his shop was still the same; perhaps a trifle dustier than it used to be, and opposite his counter there was a new cabinet screwed fast to the wall, full of brilliant sea-shells, starfish and horseshoe crabs, dried seaweed and branches of coral. Everyone looked at this case on entering the shop,—there was something surprising and unexpected about such a collection. It suggested the South and blue seas far away.

On the third day after the Cathedral had welcomed its long absent shepherd, that prelate himself came to call upon the apothecary, arriving at the door on foot and unattended. He greeted Auclair with friendliness and took the proffered chair, admitting that he felt the summer heat in Quebec more than he used to do.

"But you yourself, Monsieur Auclair, are little altered. I rejoice to see that God has preserved you in excellent health."

Auclair hastened to bring out a glass of fortifying cordial, and the Bishop accepted it gratefully. While he drank it, Auclair regarded him. It was unfortunate that Saint-Vallier, of all men, should have grown heavy—it took away his fine carriage. His once luxuriant brown hair was thin and grey, his triangular cheeks had become full and soft, like an old woman's, and they were waxy white. Between them, the sharp chin had almost disappeared.

"I have been thinking how fortunate I shall be to have you for my neighbour once more, Monseigneur," said Auclair. "Every spring I have given some little advice to the workmen who were attending to your garden, and I have often wished you could see your shrubs coming into bloom."

The Bishop smiled faintly and shook his head.

"Ah, monsieur, I shall not live in the episcopal Palace again. Perhaps that was a mistake; I should have waited to understand the designs of Providence more perfectly."

"Not live in your own residence, Monseigneur? That will be a great disappointment to all of us. The building is in excellent condition."

The Bishop again shook his head. "I find myself too

273

poor now to maintain such an establishment. I suppose you do not know anyone who would care to rent the Palace? The rental would be very helpful to me in my present undertakings. No, I shall reside at the Hôpital Général.* My good daughters there have arranged un petit appartement of two rooms which will meet my needs very well. I shall reside with them for the remainder of my life, God willing. Their chaplain is old and must soon retire, and I shall take his place. The office of chaplain will be quite compatible with my other duties."

Auclair was amazed. "In a hospital the duties of a chaplain are considerable, are they not?"

"But very congenial to me—" (the old man folded his hands over the kerchief he had taken out to wipe his brow) —"to celebrate the morning mass for the sisters and to hear their confessions; to administer the consolations of the Church to the sick and the dying. As chaplain I shall be in daily attendance upon the unfortunate, as is my wish."

Auclair sat silent for some moments, stroking his short beard in perplexity. Evidently nothing in his former relations with Monseigneur de Saint-Vallier was a guide for future intercourse. He changed the subject and began to speak of happenings in Quebec during the Bishop's

* Some years before he sailed for France in 1700, Bishop de Saint-Vallier had founded the Hôpital Général, for the aged and incurable. The hospital still stands today, much enlarged; the wards which Saint-Vallier built and the two small rooms in which he lived until his death are unchanged.

absence, of common acquaintances who had died in that time, among them old Monseigneur de Laval.

Saint-Vallier sighed. "Would it had been permitted me to return in time to thank him for the labours he underwent for my flock during the years of my captivity, and to close his eyes at the last. I can never hope to be to this people all that my venerable predecessor became, through his devotion and his long residence among them. But I shall be with them now for as long as God spares me, and I hope to be deserving of their affection."

At this moment a countrywoman appeared at the door. She was about to withdraw when she saw what visitor the apothecary was entertaining, but the Bishop called her back and insisted that his host attend to her needs. He waited patiently in his chair while she bought foxglove water for her dropsical father-in-law, and liquorice for her baby's cough. While he was serving her, Auclair wondered how he could give a turn to the Bishop's talk and learn from him what was going on at home. When the farmer woman had gone, he took the liberty of questioning his visitor directly.

"You have been at Versailles lately, Monseigneur? And how are things there, pray tell me?"

"Very sad since the death of the young Duc and Duchesse de Bourgogne last year. The King will never recover from that double loss. In the Duc, his grandson, he foresaw a wise and happy reign for France; and the young Duchesse had been the idol of his heart ever since she first came to them from Savoie. She was the life of the Court,—as dear to Madame de Maintenon as to the King. The official mourning is over, but the Court mourns, nevertheless."

Auclair nodded. "And the King, I suppose, is an old man now."

"Yes, the King is old. He still comes down to supper to the music of twenty-four violins, still works indefatigably with his ministers; there is dancing and play and conversation in the Salle d'Apollon every evening. His Court remains the most brilliant in Europe,—but his heart is not in it. There is no one left who can charm away his years and his cares as the little Duchesse de Bourgogne did, and nothing can make him forget for one hour the death of the Duc de Bourgogne. All Christendom, monsieur, has suffered an incalculable loss in the death of that pious prince."

"They died within a few days of each other, we heard."

Saint-Vallier bowed his head. "They were buried in the same tomb, and their little son with them."

"There is still talk of poison?"

"Popular opinion accuses the Duc d'Orléans. Their second son, an infant in arms, showed the same symptoms of poisoning, but he survived."

"Ah," said Auclair, "a bad situation! The King is seventy-seven, and the Dauphin a child in arms. That will mean a long regency. I suppose the young Duc de Berry will fill that office?"

"God grant it, monsieur, God spare him!" exclaimed

the Bishop fervently. "If any mischance were to befall the Duc de Berry, then that arch-atheist and suspected poisoner the Duc d'Orléans would be regent of France!" Saint-Vallier's voice cracked at a high pitch.

Auclair crossed himself devoutly. "I should have liked to see my King once more. He has been a great King. Is he much altered in person?"

"He is old. I had a private interview with His Majesty last November, late in the afternoon, when he was taking his exercise in the Parc of Versailles. We had scarcely begun our conference when a wind arose, stripping the trees that were already half-bare. The King invited me to go indoors to his cabinet, remarking that it distressed him now to hear the autumn winds and to see the leaves fall. That seemed to me to indicate a change."

"Yes," said Auclair, "that tells a story."

"Monsieur," began the Bishop sadly, "we are in the beginning of a new century, but periods do not always correspond with centuries. At home the old age is dying, but the new is still hidden. I felt the same condition in England, during my long captivity there. There is now no figure in the world such as our King was thirty years ago. The changes in the nations are all those of the old growing older. You have done well to remain here where nothing changes. Here with you I find everything the same." He glanced about the shop and peered into the salon. "And the little daughter, whom I used to see running in and out?"

"She is married, to our old friend Pierre Charron of Ville-Marie. He has built a commodious house in the Upper Town, beyond the Ursuline convent. They are well established in the world."

"You live alone, then?"

"For part of the year. Perhaps you remember a little boy whom my daughter befriended, Jacques Gaux? His mother was a loose woman—she died in your Hôpital Général, some years ago. The boy is now a sailor, and when he is in Quebec, between voyages, he lives with me. He occupies my daughter's little chamber upstairs." Auclair pointed to the cabinet of shells and corals. "He brings me these things back from his voyages; he is in the West India trade. I should like to keep him here all the time; but his father was a sailor—it is natural."

"No," said the Bishop, "I do not recall him. But your daughter I remember with affection. Heaven has blessed her with children?"

The apothecary's eyes twinkled. "Four sons already, Monseigneur. She is bringing up four little boys, the Canadians of the future."

"Ah yes, the Canadians of the future,—the true Canadians."

There was something in Saint-Vallier's voice as he said this which touched Auclair's heart; a note humble and wistful, something sad and defeated. Sometimes a neighbour whom we have disliked a lifetime for his arrogance and conceit lets fall a single commonplace remark that shows us another side, another man, really; a man uncertain, and puzzled, and in the dark like ourselves. Had his visitor not been a Bishop, Auclair would have reached out and grasped his hand and murmured: "Courage, mon bourgeois," as he did to down-hearted patients. The two men sat together in a warm and friendly silence until Saint-Vallier rose and said he must be going. "I shall have the pleasure of confirming your grandsons, I hope? They will live to see better times than ours."

Auclair accompanied him to the door and watched him tread his way up the hill and round the turn of the street. Then he went back to his desk with the feeling that old feuds were forgotten. He would have a great deal to tell Cécile when he went to supper there tonight. She would be quicker than anyone to sense the transformation in their old neighbour, who had built himself an episcopal residence approached by twenty-four stone steps, and who now proposed to spend the rest of his life in two small rooms in the hospital out on the river Charles. To be sure, the Bishop was a little theatrical in his humility, as he had been in his grandeur; but that was his way, Auclair reflected, and, after all, nobody can help his way. If a man admits his mistakes, that is a great deal, when he is a proud man and a Dauphinois—always a stiff-necked race.

While he was closing his shop and changing his coat to go up to his daughter's house, he thought over much that his visitor had told him, and he believed that he was indeed fortunate to spend his old age here where nothing changed; to watch his grandsons grow up in a country where the death of the King, the probable evils of a long regency, would never touch them.

WILLA CATHER (1873-1947) was born near Winchester, Virginia. When she was ten, her family moved from the peace of Virginia to the wild prairies of Nebraska. She was graduated from the University of Nebraska at twenty-one, and did newspaper work and teaching in Pittsburgh, Pennsylvania, for the next few years. She published a book of verse, April Twilights, *in 1903, and a book of short stories,* The Troll Garden, *in 1905. They were followed, over the years, by twelve novels, including* Death Comes for the Archbishop *and* Shadows on the Rock; *four volumes of short stories and two volumes of essays. Willa Cather was awarded the Pulitzer Prize for fiction in 1923.*